TWO SHERPAS

First published by Charco Press 2023
Charco Press Ltd.,
Office 59, 44-46 Morningside Road, Edinburgh EH10 4BF

Copyright © Sebastián Martínez Daniell, 2018
First published in Spanish as *Dos sherpas* by Entropía (Argentina)
English translation copyright © Jennifer Croft, 2023

Work published with funding from the 'Sur' Translation Support
Programme of the Ministry of Foreign Affairs of Argentina / Obra
editada en el marco del Programa 'Sur' de Apoyo a las Traducciones del
Ministerio de Relaciones Exteriores y Culto de la República Argentina.

A CIP catalogue record for this book is
available from the British Library.

ISBN: 9781913867416
e-book: 9781913867423

www.charcopress.com

Edited by Fionn Petch
Cover designed by Pablo Font
Typeset by Laura Jones
Proofread by Fiona Mackintosh

Sebastián Martínez Daniell

TWO SHERPAS

Translated
by Jennifer Croft

CHARCO PRESS

My ear is crying.
I am going down; you should go down, too.

Nima Chhiring:
yak herder, former Sherpa

One

Two Sherpas peer into the abyss. Eyes scouring the nadir. Bodies outstretched across the rock, hands gripping the precipice's edge. They seem to be expecting something. But not anxiously. Instead, with a repertoire of serene gestures that balance between resignation and doubt.

Two

One of the Sherpas gets distracted for a minute. He's young; he's still a teenager. Nonetheless he has already summited, twice. The first time when he was fifteen; the second a few months ago. This young Sherpa doesn't wish to spend his life on Everest. He's saving up to study abroad. In Dhaka, perhaps. Or in Delhi. He's made some inquiries about enrolling in Statistics. But now, as his gaze focuses and empties out over this topographic hollowness, he fantasises that his vocation could be naval engineering. He likes boats. He's never been in one: it doesn't matter. He is fascinated by floating.

Who isn't? Who doesn't envy the jellyfish and its drift across the open sea? That sensation of going with a flow. That subtle phosphorescent unfurling, devoid of vanity; let the currents take care of the rest. To float. To disentangle yourself from the course of history; not to bear that cross. Amorality without excesses, without guilt. Blindness and bioluminescence. Tentacular electricity that discloses the dark of the ocean at night.

Three

The other Sherpa first trod the slopes of Everest five weeks after he turned thirty-three. He had arrived in Nepal six years before. With well-toned muscles but no advanced knowledge of mountaineering. Some previous experience, yes, but disjointed, lacking structure or specific training. Since his baptism as a Sherpa, he's attempted to reach the summit four times. On none of those occasions has he made it to the top. Not necessarily through any fault of his own, or not always. But this recurring deferral explains to some extent why his next gesture goes a little further: beyond doubt and into irritation. *Tourists…* thinks the old Sherpa, who isn't old or, properly speaking, a Sherpa. *They always manage to do something, these people – these tourists,* he thinks. Then says. With an ambiguous gesture, he indicates the void, the ledge where the body of an Englishman lies prone and immobile, and he says:

'These people…'

And so he breaks the silence. If the deafening noise of the wind ravelling over the ridges of the Himalayas can be considered silence.

People from the East

Five hundred years prior, a nomadic people with a tradition of seasonal migration across the central Chinese province of Sichuan initiates a process of gradual westerly motion. In exile, they become pariahs: refugees who must seek their new station in the mountains. The locals baptise them according to their cardinal origins. People (*pa*) from the East (*Shar*): Sherpas.

Five

'These people…' says the old Sherpa.

And with that – that grimace of contempt, that gesture, that intonation, the astringent way he has of getting his two words off his chest – he reveals a couple of particularities: his age, which isn't so advanced; his experience, which is relatively scant; but also his sorrow, his aversion, and his licence, issued by the Ministry of Culture, Tourism, and Civil Aviation, his official permission to guide foreign visitors on their ascent of the highest mountain on the planet, the seal of approval from those offices in Kathmandu, that bureaucratic endorsement.

Six

The young Sherpa was four when his father died.

'There was an incident with the forklift,' is what he's been told his whole life. 'In the council warehouse, as they were loading up the Caterpillar parts.'

Now he hears the old Sherpa saying:

'These people…'

And, although it's unclear if he's the intended recipient of this brief message, he nods at once. A gesture of understanding, of empathy.

Seven

If someone were to pose the question – if at this very moment a person were to come up on this cliff and distract the old Sherpa from his abstraction, redirect for a moment the old Sherpa's gaze from the ledge where the Englishman is lying still; if some curious spirit were to tap him on the shoulder, requiring him to turn around, and were then to ask him what he thought about bureaucracy – the old Sherpa would come out with something unexpected: he would say that bureaucrats are holy men.

Versions of Buddhism

One of the hypotheses on the migration of the Sherpas suggests they were expelled from the Sichuan prairies for religious reasons. The Sherpas were Buddhists of the Mahayana variety, more secular and less dogmatic than the Theravada branch. For fourteen hundred years, both schools coexisted in relative harmony: they shared their monasteries and their reading of the sutras. But at some point in the fifteenth century, and somewhere in China, the factions radicalised. The Mahayana Buddhists believed that it was possible to democratise Nirvana. That just about anyone could achieve a state of enlightenment. Like Zen doctrine, which owes much of its cosmological framework to it, the Mahayana interpreted Buddhism as method rather than as worship. The Theravada, meanwhile, had a more restrictive idea of the proper path: you'd need to lead a monastic life, in absolute asceticism, and maintain a monomaniacal dedication to the precepts of Siddhartha Gautama in order to complete your journey. Wisdom, then, for the Theravada: in the hands of a religious caste, exclusive, hierarchical. There was no room for the uninitiated. Consequently, and to summarise, the Mahayana were cut off in the monasteries and cast out of society. Marginalised in Sichuan, they began heading west, into the mountains – into the Himalayas.

Nine

The bureaucrat? A conservative, of course, like anyone canonised. A hinderer. That's what the old Sherpa would say. And at the same time: a holy man. A guardian, the Grail's custodian, a Joseph of Arimathea eternalised in his crypt of laws, edicts, and amendments, provisions and standardised protocols all in keeping with arbitrary norms: therein lies their value. That's the key, the old Sherpa would point out. The arbitrariness.

The bureaucrat has been toppled over into the watery well of disgrace, the old Sherpa would say. He has been subjected to the notion – now irreversibly disseminated – that a bureaucrat is a device – half-human, half-anonymous, entirely impersonal – whose mission is to encumber the lives of free souls. A sly Leviathan that takes pleasure in crushing the citizen-insect. And the apathetic citizens and the witless insects are like so many bits of crystal – delicate, fragile, and above all sensitive, so sensitive – that wind up pulverised by the machinery of all-powerful intrigue.

We have to understand, the old Sherpa would continue – in a calmer tone – that behind the bureaucrat there's something both substantial and ungraspable:

something that one minute offers shelter to those on the street, that feeds them, and clothes them; and the next minute transforms into a terrifying apparatus, a creature with wild claws that spreads plagues and conflagrations, magnicides. One minute it represents the pinnacle of gregarious engineering, the most refined Apollonian mechanism of social regulation; the next it's a groping homunculus spewing pus and other people's blood onto the last remnants of a massacred autonomy.

Good thing there's no one to come up to him, no one to inquire about bureaucracy, no one to distract him from the contemplation of that British body which lies eight or ten metres below; its head pointing west, its legs south, for the most part, although really in every direction.

Ten

"Scene one. A street in Rome. Flavius, Marullus, a mob of citizens. An initial division has already occurred. On one side, we have two tribunes, two officials who have benefited from the class system of this empire. We can assume they are elegantly dressed; with their noses in the air. On the other side, some anonymous persons: First Commoner, Second Commoner, prisoners of a nomenclature lacking in specificity. In some versions they are described by their profession; in none by their proper names. There is more. The two tribunes are upset. Meanwhile, the plebeians celebrate. We already know all this, and they haven't even opened their mouths yet.

"Flavius breaks the enchantment. He looks out at the crowd and says, 'Hence!' In other words: 'Get out of here!' The tribune orders; the citizens listen. Flavius continues: 'Home, you idle creatures, get you home!' Flavius wants the citizens to return to their homes; he reproaches them for their vagrancy, reminds them that it's prohibited to circulate in the street without guild identification. 'Is this a holiday?' he asks them. He doesn't wait for a reply. 'A labouring day', he answers.

"And so we have an outline of our Flavius already:

elitist, demanding, authoritarian. Why? Where did he get such a feeling of impunity? Who does he think he is to talk to the plebeians that way? How dare he expel these citizens from the very streets of Rome?"

Eleven

Another time – April, prolegomenon to the high season – an avalanche: fourteen thousand tons of ice; sixteen dead. All Sherpas.

Twelve

Extracurricular activities in secondary schools in the village of Namche, at the foot of Mount Everest, begin in October, a few weeks after the start of the regular school year. Such that the young Sherpa has been taking the theatre workshop for seven and a half months. Although – strictly speaking – we would have to subtract from that count the twenty-one days that he's been on this expedition, and the five weeks of a previous ascent. It should be understood that climbing licences are a common phenomenon in the Nepalese school system: the Ministry of Education periodically prints supplements so that students who earn their keep as mountain guides can catch up with their classmates. That isn't the young Sherpa's problem. He has accumulated more than enough academic merit to resolve the curriculum without impediment. His concern is something else: the annual objective of the theatre workshop.

Perhaps presumptuous, perhaps excessive, the plan is to stage a version of *Julius Caesar* in the third week of June. The original work, which was written by Shakespeare in the final year – it is believed – of the sixteenth century, requires the participation of over two score performers.

More modestly, the drama teacher at the Namche public high school has improvised an adaptation that can be staged with the limited human resources available: the seventeen students in the class. The solutions the teacher has come up with are partly dramaturgic and partly demographic. On one hand, numerous characters' lines have been absorbed by other characters. On the other, almost everyone has to play more than one role over the course of the performance.

Memorising the lines of two or even three different characters is no small feat for a teenager with only rudimentary training in acting. But the young Sherpa has been shown some mercy here. Being the newest student in the workshop and the only one who has to face making his stage debut, he has had the good fortune to land a very simple role: Flavius, a less-than-supporting character who appears in just one scene. There is, however, a catch. That exclusive intervention occurs at the opening of the first scene of the first act. The moment the curtain is drawn and, in the dark, the audience falls into the most ominous of silences.

Wakefulness

Where did this old Sherpa come from? What is his background? What's he doing here, gazing into the void, on a mountain at such a great remove? That's what the young Sherpa wonders as he watches him, focused on his contemplation of the Englishman below. Meanwhile, the young Sherpa knows exactly where he himself has come from. From his house, in Namche, very nearby. The young Sherpa also thinks that he could do an exact and exhaustive review of his own genealogy and background.

For example, that second-to-last day of winter: March 19, a childhood Monday. It began with an anomaly. The young Sherpa – five years old, pure potential – awoke before dawn broke over the mountain range. He then remained unsleeping. It wasn't worry. Nor was it a nightmare. Merely the impulse of a body that was ready to forsake the horizontal, to be wakeful, to synthesise some carbohydrates. He lay there for a while with his eyes open, perusing the grey contours of nocturnality, the silhouette of his surrendered sister on the mat to his side. That filled him with calm but not with languor. He sat up, arms stretched out behind him, hands resting against his sheet. He stayed like that for a few minutes, taking stock of his options. Eventually he got up and silently walked to the window. He opened the curtain a crack: a fragment of sky, a yellowish lamp post, insects on their clamorous quest to seduce the streetlights. The situation as novel and ambiguous. On one hand, a slight excitement, the feat of being the one person awake in the house, or in all of Namche, perhaps. A sensation that returned throughout childhood: the feeling of being exceptional. Of being the anointed one, that figure always so abused by mythical and commercial narratives. So the young Sherpa, focusing with all of his five years, stared at the broken horizon of the mountain to ward off the sun's emergence and felt important. Even though, at the same time, there was also a vague anxiety, a feeling of vulnerability. Eagerness to put an end to that dislocated epic and run straight for his mother's big mattress. Eiderdown and immaturity. To return to a prior state, less autonomous, more comfortable. To surrender to the heat around his mother's body; to take advantage of her slumber. Perhaps if he had been a little colder, or a couple of years younger... He did not give in to the temptation: the young Sherpa was always a pragmatic child. He still is. He continued looking out the window. A bat flew past, a little one. The young Sherpa yawned and heard noises. It was his mother getting up, her steps, the door to the bathroom, that flush. The young Sherpa was overcome by guilt that had no basis: he was innocent of every crime. Except for wakefulness. But he felt like he'd been caught. He ran barefoot to his own mat and lay down as his mother came out of the bathroom. He stayed still. Face against the pillow, senses alert. Breathing as the only leakage; breathing: inevitable steady emanation. He pretended he was asleep. He imagined he was sleeping. Until he fell asleep.

Fourteen

The old Sherpa keeps his worries quiet. *These people…* They call us 'Sherpas', he thinks and lifts his chin. *Up here, they're polite. They smile at us and call us 'Sherpas'. That gives us a certain distinction, recognises some degree of expertise in us…*

Now the old Sherpa spits, with force, and the saliva is carried away by the wind, falling fast on far-off snow. Although distances are difficult to estimate on the mountain. The lack of reference points, the abstract plane of a cloudless sky, the absence of movement.

…Up here they call us Sherpas, thinks the old Sherpa: *but when they're in their homes, with their shoes off, sliding around on their parquet floors in their woollen slippers… when they've turned on their central heating, set their thermostat to exactly where they want it, when they've got food in the oven and their bodies are being traversed by high-frequency microwaves…* The old Sherpa pauses here to mentally compose a picture of an apartment with generous ceilings and curtained picture windows, polished pitch pine, a hi-fi system that doesn't disturb the neighbours but that does blanket the room in sound. What's playing? Satie? Gurdjieff? That's what comes to his mind at first. But he thinks he shouldn't go

that far, get that carried away. It could be jazz, although that would be a bit broad. He needs something else... *World music,* that's what's on! Senegalese percussion or, at the height of ironic gesture, a litany by Tibetan monks. Religious mantras of the mountain, digitalised, having lost their dynamic range and, along the way, all mysticism, too. A sophisticated straying. No need to resort to the iconography of the nouveau riche. He imagines neither terraces open to the warm Malibu air nor importuning in the mansions of Saint Petersburg.

No: the old Sherpa evades the temptation of caricature. He visualises a spacious apartment, white walls hung with Turner reproductions, high-backed armchairs. Europe, of course. Never the plebeian Americas, nor plundered Africa. Nor Asian capitals, which have as many branchings as there are roots sunk into the earth. The picture windows, the pitch pine, the Turner, the guttural sound of Tibet! We're in Europe, where else.

Fifteen

There is a second historical explanation for the Sherpas' migration. There are those who believe they left Sichuan in search of professional opportunities. They abandoned their shepherding and set off along the road of salt and silk. The course of European commerce, the wake of the commercial greed of the West, which profited by putting spices in the kitchens of Renaissance palaces. According to this other hypothesis, the Sherpa population was born in the heat of the anthropocentric revolution of Dürer, Petrarch, and Francis Bacon. Children of the early bourgeoisie, the Sherpas reinvent themselves as means of transport, as freight for exchangeable goods.

Afghan greyhounds, Ankara cats

The old Sherpa thinks: *When they're in their European rooms, releasing the barely perceptible vapours from their glasses of brandy, when they're brushing their Afghan greyhounds, when they're petting their Ankara cats… That's when we stop being Sherpas and start being 'porters'. Porters!*

He pauses in order to give himself room to savour his resentment, to position the sound of the word in his inner ear. *That's what they call us when we're not around: 'Porters'.* He goes further: *Beasts of burden. As necessary and at the same time as interchangeable as pitons, as harnesses, as rope.*

Seventeen

It is early on the mountainside. The two Sherpas lower their eyes until they see the Englishman. All three bodies fall still again. Time passes. It's hard to say how much. Or how. Until the young Sherpa gets distracted: *Naval engineering? Why not?* It strikes him as a good idea. He has a mind like a sponge when it comes to maths. His teachers have told him this. He makes a quick calculation: he'll finish high school in a year, then go to university in Delhi, or in Dhaka, or at the Bombay Institute of Technology; he'll get his diploma four years later; he'll go to graduate school, specialised training in London, or Tokyo. At twenty-six he could be working a port in the Indian Ocean. Or in the China Sea. Even Europe. His English isn't bad. Neither is his French. He has a gift for languages, all his teachers have told him so. *Naval engineering... I could work in the port of Lisbon*, he thinks. He doesn't know a word of Portuguese; he doesn't care. Lisbon: he imagines it open, cast into the Tagus estuary, exotic and wild.

Eighteen

"But Flavius doesn't only want to cast the citizens of Rome out of the streets. He also wants to know why he's doing it. To this end, he asks one of the craftsmen: 'Speak, what trade art thou?' 'Why, sir, a carpenter,' the man answers. Marullus, the other tribune, a bit more limited than Flavius, joins in on the harassment. 'Where is thy leather apron and thy rule?' he chides the carpenter. He turns to someone else: 'You, sir, what trade are you?' But this time it's not so simple. This second citizen responds evasively. He doesn't quite specify his occupation. He gives the tribune to understand that he repairs things, that he's a repairer. He does throw in a few key words, like *mender of bad soles.* But Marullus doesn't seem to want to get it; he refuses. He's not one for hermeneutics, not even the simplest kind. He gets angry and demands the man speak clearly. This man will not be intimidated, though. He takes it all with a grain of salt, with humour, even: he tells the tribune not to be out of sorts on his account, although, he says, if he does get bent out of shape, then he can surely fix him.

"There is a psychic distance then (upset versus cheerfulness) that threatens to deteriorate into linguistic rift (literality versus playful popular obliteration). But in that moment the State finds the way: Flavius, your Flavius, our Flavius. More phlegmatic, less aggressive, our tribune understands everything: 'Thou art a cobbler, art thou?' he asks. Exactly, complete decryption. So he moves on. 'But wherefore art not in thy shop today? Why dost thou lead these men about the streets?' he asks. 'Truly, sir, to wear out their shoes, to get myself into more work,' responds the cobbler. Yet again he privileges business, profitability. Citizens mutate into merchants in pursuit of economic gains. For a moment, Flavius' attitude grows benign, and the road to open conversation appears to be clear.

"But it's only a flicker, an almost imperceptible relaxation of the muscles of his forehead. Because immediately the cobbler confesses: 'But indeed, sir, we make holiday to see Caesar and to rejoice in his triumph.' The people will celebrate their Caesar. The tribunes will not. The tribunes hold this Caesar in contempt. They venerate Pompey yet: their assassinated leader. More distance now. 'And do you now strew flowers in his way that comes in triumph over Pompey's blood?' asks Marullus, reproaching the citizens their latest loyalty.

"Up until this point, everything is going as we might expect. But suddenly, implausibly, Marullus and Flavius convince the craftsmen to return to their homes, to apologise to the gods, to shed tears in the Tiber for Pompey and to abjure the cause of Julius. And they ('See whe'er their basest mettle be not moved,' as Flavius puts it) all exit. They empty the streets."

Nineteen

The old Sherpa breaks the silence once more. He points to the abyss and to the Englishman who is its decoration.

'Why won't he do anything? He could cry out, at least.'

The old Sherpa wants the Englishman to scream, to get up, to get on a plane where he can run afoul of the flight attendants… Anything for him to drop the mineral attitude he has now. But that doesn't seem to be an option for him. What he can do, it seems, is lie there Britishly upon the mountain. Detach himself from disquiet and its retinue of shallow breaths, blank stares, and self-satisfaction. The Sherpa would like for it to rain, at least. Hard. Big, fat drops. Let the sidewalks of the cities flood, the storm drains overflow; let pluvial ducts be insufficient in their underground array.

The young Sherpa hears the old man despair at the Englishman's lack of reaction, and he nods. He gazes into the obscene transparency of the oxygen-poor air, and he nods.

He would have liked to tell the older man about his thoughts on naval engineering. Ask him for his opinion and find acceptance in it, feel his enthusiasm being fed back. But he knows there isn't any point with the old Sherpa. He recalls when he told him he wanted to study History of Law. The older man did not take that well. The greater part of his response was unintelligible. Now he senses – or rather fears – that something similar will happen. He senses – or fears – that the old Sherpa will tell him that a boy raised in the mountains could never establish an intuitive relationship with the sea. That that shortcoming would cause him insurmountable problems designing ships, submarines, oil platforms, or whatever it is naval engineers do. He senses – or fears – that the old man will raise his voice. That he'll shout: 'Idiotic caprice!' That he'll mock: 'A boy who has never in his life set foot outside Nepal intends to launch his career in the ocean…' That he'll conclude: 'You were born with a seven-hundred-kilometre restraining order on your head, issued by the ocean. What do you think the damned ocean is? I actually know what it's like, and I can assure you it's not how you imagine it.' The old man could well say all of that. And, given the choice, the young Sherpa prefers to avoid making scenes.

Which is why he keeps his ideas about his vocational options to himself. Decides, instead of sharing, to silently nod. Let that silence speak for him. If the thunderous noise of the wind crossing the ridges of the Himalayas can be considered silence.

It's not like he lacks arguments, of course. At this very moment, in a muted hypothetical argument against his colleague's imagined objections, he thinks that he has seen the ocean countless times. For starters, on TV. And, although it should go without saying, online. And, since he was very young, in photographs at school. He has seen it from every possible angle: from faded images of sunsets over the Pacific to bathyscaphe expeditions in the Mariana Trench. He is practically an expert on the ocean, the young Sherpa now believes. And that thought, in conjunction with that show of restraint, that control over what he keeps to himself and what he does not say, lends him courage, a kind of new confidence in himself. An impulse that leads him to tap the older man's shoulder and say something – something else, something new, unrelated to the Englishman or to naval engineering. He shifts onto his knees and asks:

'Shall we get up?'

Parasols

Of the young Sherpa's father, only the photos remain. All the ones his mother treasures in a thermal boot box, filed away above the wardrobe, and the three that are framed and displayed for all to see.

In one of these, his parents are on one of the beaches of Digha. Their honeymoon. In the background, coloured parasols, people lying in the sand. Multitudes. Beyond, the sea, the horizon, clouds. There is something about the arrangement of their bodies that suggests that his mother and his father barely knew each other when the photograph was taken. That it had only been a few months since the first time they spoke in the hallways of Namche's administration building: he as a worker for the Directorate of Roadways and Paths; she as a clerk at the Tourist Information desk. The young Sherpa, of course, had not been born the day that photograph was taken. His older sister hadn't, either. These absences disturb him.

Twenty-One

'Yes,' answers the old Sherpa and looks down: the Englishman's body is still there, still unmoving. How long has it been? How many minutes since the Englishman slipped, lost his balance, and, instead of obediently letting himself fall onto the ground, flapped his arms like a stork in heat, attempting to cling onto verticality until, lured in by the abyss, he fell three metres or seven metres or eleven metres onto a ledge. When did that happen? The old Sherpa estimates it was around ten minutes ago. He ought to have looked at his watch at the exact instant of the fall. But, in his confusion, time retreated to a supporting plane. Making this a solely spatial event, a Euclidian instant.

It's good to be able to count on a physical manifold, as pogroms against otherness, against difference, are carried out in our vast silicon kingdom. The Sherpa gets up, his left knee protesting.

Twenty-Two

Once established in the region of Tibet and Nepal, the Sherpa ethnic group began to gain intimate knowledge of the mountain. Exploring it, traversing it, subverting it. The group's customs started to change. Having left behind bucolic nature, they became one with the steep slopes of the mountains. They even deconstructed Buddhism's original sobriety to move towards a new theocratic version of the universe: more baroque, more imaginative, colourful. They peopled their religion with local deities and shamanic variations. Mount Everest, for instance, was called – against all phallocratic intuition – 'the mother of the world'. The giantess. It was in these first centuries of inhabiting the Himalayan territories that the Sherpas developed a physiological ability to commune with that mineral resplendence. Since then, the mountain has alerted them to imminent danger. Such premonitions are experienced as a high-pitched buzzing that arises, inexplicable, over the range. They call it *kan runu*, or: the ear that cries.

It is not, it must be said, an infallible system. Neither of the two Sherpas, not the young one nor the old one, perceived even the slightest buzz at the critical moment when an Englishman stumbled over the edge of the mountain and, with nothing to mitigate his fall, crashed against the very ledge where, even now, his body lies ambiguous, disjointed but present, waiting for the situation to be defined in these its silent surrounds. If the thundering monochord whistling of the incessant gusts of air that cut through the high peaks of the Himalayas can be considered silence.

A silence, in short, similar to the one the young Sherpa will hear in a month when he steps on stage for the first time and, facing the darkness of his audience, is forced to pronounce the first line of *Julius Caesar.*

'Hence! Home, you idle creatures, get you home!'

Melting

Few clouds in the sky. And an already weak troposphere that tends towards consumption. The sun dominates the slope of Everest, then, and the command of its radiations. Some of the snow gets exhausted and creates a liquid epidermis over the mountain. The two Sherpas have accepted that melt: it is time. (And in any case their eyes are on the immobile body of the Englishman.) But, glimpsed from a different distance, the thaw is no less virulent because it happens daily: the inapprehensible energy, the frenzy of those molecules, the degradation of atomic alliances defeated by heat...

The young Sherpa's trousers get damp at the knee that's on the ground, and in that moment, he says to his partner:

'Shall we get up?'

Twenty-Four

In 1909, the Pennsylvanian Robert Peary assured the world that he had managed to reach the North Pole. An unverifiable statement, almost certainly fictitious, but one that – at the time – was taken very seriously. In fact, it was the news that led Roald Amundsen to cancel a series of complicated plans that would have taken him into the Arctic and instead announce that the goal of his next expedition would be the South Pole. On 14 December 1911, then, Amundsen raised the blue and red flag of his homeland at the southernmost point on the planet, where all meridians meet. An American in the North; a Norwegian in Antarctica.

And England? Nothing. Or worse than nothing: the tragic epic of Robert Scott, who arrived at the South Pole five weeks late and proceeded to freeze to death with four other Englishmen in the midst of that Antarctic nullity. 'These rough notes and our corpses should tell the story,' Scott wrote in the last entry of his logbook. It is as if the Anglican god abandoned the islands with the death of Queen Victoria.

At least until the aristocrat Francis Younghusband proclaimed that there was still a portion of the world to deflower with the imperial flag: the umpteenth home of the Union Jack ought to be Mount Everest. This notion became a matter of State. In 1921, a first expedition was launched. The mountaineer George Mallory was a member of the team. They studied the terrain, noted its challenges, decided to go home and get better prepared. The following year, they made a second attempt. One group made it to 8,300 metres. Monsoon season was just about to begin. An avalanche occurred. For a few hours, chaos reigned. The expedition sent a brief message to Base Camp to reassure their companions: 'All the whites are safe,' it says. Seven Sherpas died buried in the snow.

Ninety-three years later: 18 April, 2014. Another avalanche. Fourteen thousand tons of ice; sixteen dead. All Sherpas.

Twenty-Five

The old Sherpa is uncomfortable. It's understandable: he is, by far, the oldest member of the expedition and yet he is also not the most experienced. The boy to his right now stretching his legs knows the mountain much better, has participated in more ascents and, as if that weren't enough, has already summited twice. If everything were going well, there wouldn't be an issue. But in a crisis, which of them gets the last word? The mountaineer with the most training or the one who's spent the most time on this Earth? Do a few more years in the Himalayas give the young Sherpa superior authority to settle a quandary? For now, the old Sherpa listens to his colleague's suggestion.

'Yes,' he says and stands up. His left knee creaks.

And now that he is seeing him at the same altitude, his circulatory system readjusting its flow to correspond to this new posture of the body, his perception changes. There are no more professional misgivings, nor is there any sense of competition. All he sees is a promising, responsible young man: a partner, a good kid. To say that he loves him like a son would be preposterous. The old Sherpa knows not the mysteries of fatherhood.

But he recognises underneath the balaclava an affinity, an affection, even some degree of commitment. A connection, yes, a bond that might broaden or deepen, or both.

Light Bulbs

Periodically, after dinner, the young Sherpa's mother announces that it is time to do the household accounts. Each month the ritual repeats: going over the amounts that have come in and the inevitable expenditures. In even-numbered months, it's his sister's turn to help. But March is the domain of the young Sherpa. It is now, and it was back when he was nine years old and talented at algebra.

So their mum would put on her glasses, and he would hold on to the calculator. Their mother would hand him the notebook, the spiralled spine of a Precambrian animal, and he would sharpen the pencil with a razor blade that had been kept in the medicine cabinet since the incident with the Caterpillar. Then he would listen, record and add and subtract, trusting in the graphite that ran over the page like a herd of bison.

'We need to consume less electricity,' their mother would admonish. 'I don't understand how it can cost so much if our bulbs are always burning out.'

Nobody answered her; they took it for granted that she was right; who could understand, after all, the breakdown of the utility bills printed in Kathmandu that the mail would leave sporadically, unpredictably outside their door.

The rite of accounting completed, the young Sherpa would place all the bills in a moss-green folder, and he'd place the folder next to the notebook in the dresser drawer. He'd ask if he could take to school that same pencil he still had in his hand because the one in his pencil case was already very short, having been so used up that now his fingers all came together around the point, to the detriment of his handwriting. His mother would nod, already half asleep, so the young Sherpa would rummage around in his backpack until he hit upon the pencil case and put the new pencil next to the consumed one. Just in case, he would not discard the older pencil: who knew, academic life worked through the accumulation of imponderables.

'Isn't your backpack too heavy, son?' his mother would say, rising from her chair: she was always worrying about a cervical deformity befalling the young Sherpa.

'But I have to carry it; I've got everything in there.'

'You're going to end up a hunchback,' she'd say, but the admonition was already losing steam, more formal than programmatic.

'No, mum. That's because my mat is too soft,' the young Sherpa would repeat something his older sister had told him.

'Fine, take a bath,' his mother would say, and go into her room to put on her light blue nightgown.

'Yes,' the young Sherpa would answer and go into the bathroom, turn on the shower, a vague and lukewarm stream, with no digressions or conical expansions, thudding onto the ceramic floor tiles. Something to do with the pressure, or lack of pressure, or the malfunctioning of the shower. A hypotensive bath. First he'd wash his hair, not too efficiently. He would lather up his body and try not to make noise. In spite of everything, the water was warmish, and he had no desire to leave it.

That was why the young Sherpa dallied in the bathroom by the light of the filament of a small bulb that would be the next one to burn out. One of the household chores he'd been assigned since earliest childhood was changing the light bulbs. And putting away the dishes his mother would wash after dinner. His homework always came last. He'd do it already on his mat, with the light that came in the window from the street as sole illumination. But he hadn't got to that part of the day yet. For now, he was taking a shower. The scenery in the bathroom matched his mood: lunar tundra amidst flashes of quasars.

Lichen

On the mountain, the vegetable kingdom has limited options. The lack of oxygen imposes ineluctable restrictions. Lichen is the mountaineer's only companion, encouraging him to lick the rock in accordance with the maximalist postulate that life is stronger than nothingness. In its double scaffolding of fungus and alga, two-faced Janus of the botanical order, with its effective alliance against sterility, lichen colonises, dominates the high peaks. But it is a king without subjects: it has sovereignty, it has territory, but its dominion is diluted in the vastness of mineral abstraction. There are microorganisms, of course. But there is no merit in subduing those too weak to depose us. It is said that there are lichens that survive even suspension in the cosmic void. There is no reason to disbelieve this. But lichen desires something else. Its pride is not resistance to hostility, but rather expansion – imperial lust.

The same could be said for the climbers. What purpose could they have in throwing themselves into an unnatural ascent towards the unbreathable summit of the Himalayas? What is the point in exhausting your capabilities, getting distracted, staggering, and hurtling eight, eleven, twelve metres just to crash onto a ledge? It isn't self-improvement, as they try to claim. Quite the contrary, to best themselves would be to dispense with their objectives. What they're really seeking is the illusion of subjugation. Egomaniacs, naïfs – and especially those who fall under the record-holding influence of Everest – yearn to dominate the vacuum. And they fail. Whether they give up or they summit, they always fail.

Meanwhile, the Sherpa is Zarathustra. For him the important part starts when he's coming back down from the mountain. Filled with rage and without any trace of mercy. Like the German philologist, he knows that if he gazes into the abyss for long enough, he'll catch the abyss gazing back.

Twenty-Eight

It is a moment of introspection; the two Sherpas stretching their joints: the younger with a twist of the neck to ward off future cramps, the older with his eyes on his colleague, with a hint of precognitive nostalgia, as if already taking responsibility for a farewell, a bifurcation in their futures, one that is still remote, but also unavoidable. Neither speaks.

Outstanding

The young Sherpa is a good student, that much is clear. An alert and curious teenager. Perhaps he hasn't applied himself completely, perhaps he isn't a fanatic of curricular obligations, but nonetheless a student without any major obstacles on his academic journey. Above average, it could be said. Perhaps not the most spectacular of the crop. Yet undoubtedly someone who easily passes the vast majority of his exams, not to mention his homework, and all the other booby traps of student life. In fact, as he contemplates, from a standing position now, the static figure of the Englishman sprawled across a grizzled crag of the Himalayas, he takes the opportunity to go over the list of outstanding assignments that he will need to present to his teachers when he gets down from the mountain. And he thinks for a moment about his sister, who ought to be at home by now. And about his father, who is gone. He also thinks about his mother, who at this time would be behind the counter of the Tourist Service desk, in accordance with the schedule imposed on her by the town council of Namche.

Thirty

"And so Flavius walks with Marullus through the streets of Rome. Are they equals? Nominally, it could be said that they are: two tribunes, two followers of Pompey, two opponents of Julius Caesar. Yet a chasm yawns between them. Where Marullus is impulsive and lacking in tact, constrained in his understanding, Flavius is shrewd and efficient. Less charismatic, perhaps, but more managerial. They walk, as we were saying, through the streets of Rome. They come upon a mob of citizens celebrating the Caesar's return. They admonish the crowd, reproach them for their enthusiasm: 'Wherefore rejoice?' Marullus asks these ordinary Romans. Then he accuses them of being traitors, or, more precisely, turncoats: 'Knew you not Pompey? Many a time and oft have you climbed up to wall and battlements, to towers and windows, yea, to chimney tops, your infants in your arms, and there have sat the livelong day, with patient expectation, to see great Pompey pass the streets of Rome.' Marullus says this while Flavius keeps quiet. And this matters because a kind of moral double-dealing reigns over this section and its forms. Here Marullus recognises that the questionable thing is not citizens going out into the streets to celebrate the triumph of Rome's leader on a labouring day and without the signs of their profession. The problem is that they are doing all of this for Julius. When they did it for Pompey it was perfectly acceptable, a deserved veneration. You must remember, young actor, that between Plutarch and Shakespeare, history had already ensured that Pompey was placed on the pedestal of beautiful forms. Pompey, the Apollonian; Julius, the Dionysian. Pompey, the man of prudence; Julius, the man of excess. Or, as Marullus tells those Caesar-loving citizens regarding Pompey: 'And when you saw his chariot but appear, have you not made a universal shout, that Tiber trembled underneath her banks to hear the replication of your sounds made in her concave shores?' Marullus gets choked up when he remembers those bygone days. Maybe Flavius would not have got so emotional. But his companion is made of more combustible stuff. Marullus launches his final attack against the mob: 'And do you now strew flowers in his way that comes in triumph over Pompey's blood? Be gone! Run to your houses, fall upon your knees, pray to the gods to intermit the plague that needs must light on this ingratitude.'

"And having come to this point, and before the whole play turns into too much of a bore, Flavius has to intervene, add a dash of reason to the whole. He interrupts Marullus and, being more of a mending type himself, he tells the citizens: 'Go, go, good countrymen.' He's a wily one, that Flavius. Marullus, a maniac, calls them ingrates and traitors and sinners. But Flavius calls them 'good countrymen' and gets them on his side: they share this country, and they are equal in the eyes of Rome. But his cunning does not stop there. Immediately he tells them something else: 'For this fault assemble all the poor men of your sort; draw them to the Tiber banks, and weep your tears into the channel, till the lowest stream do kiss the most exalted shores of all.' In one fell swoop, the 'countrymen' become 'poor men', persons classified by their 'sort'. But that's a minor detail. The central thing in Flavius' speech is that he summons the plebs, the same people who cheered for Caesar seconds earlier, to disseminate the interests of the Senate. He wins them over to his cause and puts them on the campaign trail."

The Farm

The young Sherpa wonders: how has it never occurred to him, despite having spent so much time on Mount Everest with this older man, to find out why he decided to come all the way to Nepal?

The young Sherpa knows exactly where he himself comes from. He thinks that he could, if he wanted to, reconstruct each and every trace of his passage through the world so far. His birth in a public hospital, the yak wool blankets from the first two winters, the formula and his big sister's efficient custody, the bleeding wounds of childhood, his education…

The morning of the field trip to the farm, to take just one example. He recalls it perfectly. The premise – the promise – was that they'd see animals whose nature had been altered by domestication. Going the opposite way from the tourists: down the mountain, the stony path, the thistles of the foothills. Reaching a valley and then the countryside, a farm, or something like it: indeterminate, pastoral; a little green, a lot of children, mud from all the thaws.

The young Sherpa – eight at the time – had been nursing exaggerated expectations. Then again that was childhood, or at least it was his: a constant assemblage of outrageous predictions, a permanent fleeing from the referential framework. He didn't even know what he might find on a farm. But he assumed it was something wild, indomitable. The very thing that would bring about the greatest unpredictability. Fantasies of piracy punctuated his anticipation. Not Caribbean piracy, but South Pacific: a Malay tint to them, or one of Indochina, scimitars, pets with feral fangs, airs of illegality. He didn't want to leave these images behind; eight years, stubbornness, and the young Sherpa made strenuous efforts not to allow those ideas out of his head, because the way they were, immaculate, with a hint of typhoon or electricity, they kept him bristling.

He could also describe in detail the journey to the farm, which began when the teacher stood at the door, straightened out an irregular line of children and gave the command for them to start walking. A hallway, a courtyard, the school gate, the exterior. Then they stopped a moment. The teacher's voice reminded them: 'You already know Raju, our bedel. Raju is going to accompany us on our excursion today. Listen to him. Is everybody ready? Does anybody need to go to the bathroom?'

The young Sherpa remembers everything. For instance, that the first thing he tried to do was figure out if he already knew Raju. Raju's features struck him as familiar but far away, from another time. That is if childhood recognises other times. The young Sherpa scratched his knee and looked at the back of the bedel's neck, his dark hair divided by the line of a baseball cap. It wasn't like the hair on the back of his father's neck, so carefully, evenly trimmed. It was quite different, in fact. *Papa's neck was more like mine*, thought the young Sherpa, although he had a very vague image of the back of his own neck. No one has an exact idea of their own occipital measure. You'd need to be afflicted with a very specific type of narcissism, a literally retrospective vanity. But as three-dimensionality insists on incomplete images, it's inevitable that certain things get left in the dark. Listening is something else, you might think. But the truth is that the treble of the violin or the military whistle also conceal from us unknowable frequencies. Dogs are different: they transgress the interdiction and parade around the full width of their hearing threshold as though in celebration of some merit of their own. Whales, in their oceanic, infrasonic becoming, reproach them from the opposite end of the tonal field.

It was already getting warm, recalls the young Sherpa; all the warmth a person can sense during springtime at the base of the Himalayas. The young Sherpa went up to Raju. He wanted to learn the sound of his voice.

'Looks like it's going to be a hot one today,' he said to Raju, and he was surprised by the futile maturity of his comment. Perhaps being an adult was that: the uttering of appropriate and dead-end phrases, belonging and adaptation.

The bedel looked at him, his head pointing down, and responded perfectly naturally:

'They're predicting snow for tonight.'

Adulthood, then, was more complex: there was, as well, the sphere of confrontation. Before the young Sherpa could answer, the bedel was called into the school's interior, fleeing the scene.

Later, yes, he remembers it now, an exhausting hike all the way down the mountain. Namche has no streets or highways: just a helipad and footpaths, the meanders of ruggedness and isolation. Thus they had to leave the village, cross a bridge, climb a hill, keep walking, simulate suicides, celebrate bad jokes. And even then they were still in the immediate vicinity. But we ought not imagine a declining industrial periphery, nor that indefinable geography that alternates between the primitivism of rural flora and the poverty of certain outlying areas. Namche is not Kathmandu – it's not even Darjeeling. It's just a collection of buildings given over to tourism and simple houses on steps drilled into the mountain range. Crossing the city limit consists in passing the last neighbour who lives next to a white painted stone. Beyond that is outer space.

After forty minutes of walking, after the young Sherpa had already revised his expectations – which suddenly struck him as without foundation, unjustifiable – they landed on a modest plain: the farm. Or rather, a scant lot with a few donkeys, mules, turkeys, four yaks, and a huge pig. But the visit to the farm was over in an instant, and it was time to number off, occupy positions, look straight ahead, return.

And on that ascent up the hill, the young Sherpa was for the first time – he remembers it now, facing the Englishman – suspended in the moment a forklift falls over, and a father dies. Mourning out of sync. The way back to Namche, then, a Golgotha. Valley, hill, bridge, stony path... But not the ascent of the Messiah, who knows he is predestined and reluctantly accepts his sacrificial delirium. More like the Calvary, the ordeal of the bad thief: he, too, has been whipped. Same nails, same splinters, and not even a crown.

The road back and Namche on the horizon, if a mountain range can allow for a horizon. The languor of the tail end of a party, the already vaporous memory of their excursion, and the young Sherpa hadn't asked to lose his dad. His lunch still in his backpack. He hadn't found a reason to eat it. First out of euphoria, now melancholy. What had he lost on the way to the farm, before the turkeys, the mules, that apathetic yet endearing pig? What is it he wants back now? The return weighed on him, that ascent of the mountain path, that walk home, the questions, the dinner with his family.

Thirty-Two

The old Sherpa is growing a beard. This is his custom: he starts each expedition with a close shave, in order to then perceive, over the course of the ensuing days, how his facial hair gains in density, in prominence. He says that this helps him not to get decentred, to continue believing in things, in the linear logic of time, in the sequence of causes and effects.

Thirty-Three

If his father were alive, the young Sherpa would be working in some municipal office of Namche. Like his mother does, like his dead father also did. He would work far from the hazards of the high mountain and close to the forklift that, once a week, facilitates the transport of the pieces of the Caterpillar that clears the snow from the footpaths.

The young Sherpa had rejected that family mandate the first time he saw Everest Base Camp. That day – twelve years old, his debut – he helped place the Tibetan prayer flags around the tents: blue, white, red, green, yellow. In that order: sky, air, fire, water, earth. Again and again: sceptre, wheel, lotus, lightning bolt, stone. All around the camp: humility, teaching, meditation, dedication, courage. What the tourists like to call *the Sherpas' coloured flags*.

Then he sat down and watched mesmerised as the flags waved over the snow. The wind by way of its manifestations.

Thirty-Four

Two years after the second expedition, Mallory attempted a third ascent of Everest. But before going up, and while trying to secure funding in the United States, he was asked why he cared so much about reaching the summit. 'Because it's there,' he responded. This time he took oxygen cylinders. He passed eight thousand metres without too much difficulty. At that point, Mallory bade farewell to the last Sherpas who were with him and undertook the final stage of the ascent alongside Andrew Irvine, aged twenty-two. On 8 June, 1924, they began to climb with the intention of reaching the summit that same day.

Mallory's body was recovered seventy-five years later with fractures of the femur and tibia. Irvine's is still missing. It isn't known whether they died before or after reaching the summit.

Thirty-Five

The young Sherpa has suddenly lost his penchant for naval engineering, if indeed he ever really had one. He imagined himself in a stuffy office somewhere, leaning over a tabletop from sunrise to sunset, calculating masses and resistances, responding to the demands of transnational capital, feeling overworked... Now, as he waits at the edge of a crag for something to happen with the Englishman, he thinks that perhaps it would be better to study for a diplomatic career. To travel, to defend the interests of Nepal, protect it from the greedy clutches of the rapacious world. *International relations, why not?* He's good with languages. His teachers have always said as much. He communicates in the most fluent manner with the tourists. It strikes him as an excellent plan. He has never been inside an embassy. He doesn't care: he likes the idea of geopolitics. Who doesn't? Infiltrate the ins and outs of the global engine, sit at the table with the owners of the world, feed on the very fuel that makes the planet turn. But, for fear of irritating his companion, he decides not to say any of it out loud.

Thirty-Six

The old Sherpa seems angry with the Englishman. As if falling from the mountain were a bad idea, an unfortunate occurrence evidently intended to inconvenience others. But, in order for his own bad mood not to grow contagious, he, too, decides to keep quiet, ruminating on his disapproval. Looking out over the snowy peaks of the mountain range, teeth that are decayed despite an excess of enamel.

International relations, why not? the young Sherpa wonders. Until the older man grinding his teeth brings him back to the mountain, and he looks down at the fallen tourist. This is when it starts to dawn on him that he is very close to incurring the first liability of his career. (*Liability* is one of the translations for the word the Sherpas use to refer to the tourists who perish under their care. And it is the one English-speakers appear to prefer. The French, in turn, tend to speak of *ghosts*. This might seem strange, since *ghost* and *liability* are two words that share almost no lexical paradigm. In Nepali, the original word is *hava*, which doesn't mean either of these things. It's just that the British, trained in utilitarian empiricism, immediately remitted the matter to its practical derivatives, while the French drifted off on the path of misty metaphor.)

Having a death on his record is not, of course, a good thing for a Sherpa. It is a stain on his service record. But nor does it signify the end of a career as a professional mountain guide – far from it. Sherpas are extremely supportive of colleagues who lose their tourists on the mountain. They start out from the certainty that the fault always lies elsewhere, with the foreigner who ventures out onto the slopes without sufficient preparation, or with secret suicidal tendencies. A little liability is understandable. One dead, two dead, three if they died in the same avalanche or were swallowed by the void on the same chain of harnesses. Up to that point, there would not be much cause for concern.

But it is tradition to assume that when the liabilities start to add up on a Sherpa's résumé, it does get harder and harder for him to make further ascents. It's not so much an issue of professional discredit. Superstition rules supreme upon these slopes. There's a long-standing idea that liabilities cling to Sherpas' boots, weighing them down more and more with every cadaver that piles up upon those precipices. So that, beyond any feelings of guilt (which are not among the most widespread sentiments in the Sherpa community), what worries them is myth: the intangible and intolerable oral account that claims a Sherpa with a lot of liability on his boots will eventually fall a final time, taking with him everyone he can.

Geological Pioneers

If the two Sherpas were geological pioneers, the older man would be a vulcanist, the younger man a neptunist. It would be the second half of the seventeenth century, and the task would be to put the still-unknown in order, tidy it up, establish with meticulous zest the circumscriptions of the age's ignorance. The obsessive neurosis of Linnaeus, his vanity. No more dervishes, no more Druids; no more Renaissance men soaring over the surfaces of anatomy, optics and alchemy with equal relish. The task is to establish systems. First, the stars; then organic species, and fluids, and the very passage of time. Until it's the turn of the earth sciences. Not just classifying minerals, sediments, rock strata. They must be explained: why this spiral ammonite on the slopes of the Alps? Why that mollusc in the amber emanating from that bark? All that we walk on – where is it from?

The first theory that emerges is liquid and languid; somewhat burdened by myth and, therefore, seductive, a Nereid. The ocean in retreat. An orb covered in water slowly draining away, leaving the Earth naked. Exposed to the gaze of the Creator. A world of inundations stabilising. An emerging planet that is surfacing to breathe:

whale of half an eternity of submergence. The echo of the biblical Flood and the prevalence of water as punishment that was already meted out. A totally aquatic sphere, in which the dissolved minerals keep creating solidarities until eventually they're solid. A world where firmness has had to make its own way over the course of aeons. Dryness as the conquest of time. Interesting, sure. But there is a problem with neptunism. Not where the original water came from, but where it's headed. Where is all that sea that covered the Pyrenees, the Andes, and the very Himalayas where two Sherpas peer out over a crag?

And so the rival theory: the cult of the volcanoes. Water annihilated by Hades' heat. A more violent idea, where it is incendiary lava that produces the soil. That the planet exists thanks to an incessant cycle of eruptions and cooling that guarantees its perpetuity. The centre of the world ablaze. The Earth designs its parts in the seething forge of the underworld and spits them out onto the surface via volcanoes. Matter comes out in the form of lava, cools, settles; rain and wind guide it back down to the coasts. As unrecognisable seabed, it continues to fall: gravity draws the minerals back into the inextinguishable combustion of the planetary centre, to the infernal laboratory where everything gets readulterated while awaiting another eruption. Cyclical, impetuous: this is the igneous factory of worlds that the vulcanists whipped up.

Goethe reflects the controversy in *Faust*, where it is up to Anaxagoras to argue the side of fire and to Thales, naturally, the founding role of water. 'This rock is formed by the vapour of fire,' Anaxagoras sustains. But Thales responds: 'That which lives has sprung from moisture.' Unimpressed, Anaxagoras then provokes him: 'Hast thou ever, O Thales, in one night, brought forth such a mountain out of mire?' And points out a hill we can presume to be imposing. But Thales, hydrophilic, remains collected: he tells him that nature flows, that it builds without any type of violence. So then Anaxagoras loses his patience. He says that yes, that of course there has been violence; that there was in fact a 'Plutonic angry fire' and the 'monstrous explosive power of Aeolian vapours' that 'broke through the old crust of the flat soil' so that a new mountain 'must immediately arise'. The argument continues, but this is as far as Goethe goes.

Then came science, epistemological mechanisms, Pangea, Laurasia, Gondwana, drift, the exhibitionism of the Quaternary Period. Plate tectonics are a twenti-eth-century invention, a fad imposed just forty years before the older Sherpa, vulcanist by choice, peered into the abyss alongside our young neptunist, each in contemplation of the motionless body of an Englishman.

Thirty-Eight

I *can show exactly where I'm from*, thinks the young Sherpa. Can the old man? Can he trace the ellipse that brought him to this mountain? The young Sherpa recalls another scene: something that, he thinks, serves as further proof of genealogy...

He is going home from school. He is older; he's begun attending high school. He has already seen the mountain. He's walking but decides to pause. He sits down on a stone, delaying the return. From there he can see the land that surrounds his house. In the background, the mountain range. Sterile scree everywhere. His mother emerges from the back of the house; in her arms, she holds a heavy basin. The young Sherpa sees her from the perspective of his hebetude and wants to tell her not to bother, that it will snow in the night. But she takes a couple of steps and hangs the wet clothes on the line. Using wooden pins, ligneous bamboo converted into miniature prehensiles. Above her, the elements.

Could we say *the element*? *An element*? Or is *elements* an indivisible? Can elements be fragmented, broken down into a sequence, a system and a pattern found? Or are they an ethereal creature that has no form or that assumes the endless form of what it colonises? Are they something that is there, an all-encompassing entity become chaos, something that takes in everything and always, but is nonetheless fortuitous?

If the woman said, for example, 'something dyed my clothes,' or 'something dyed my clothes almost imperceptibly,' if the young Sherpa's mother looked up, fixed her gaze on the lowering clouds, if she observed the fabric of the clothing against the glare and said aloud: 'Something dyed my clothes red so nearly imperceptibly that only I can tell,' then we would want to know: is that red, its feeble pigmentation, the elements or shelter?

The young Sherpa's mother finishes hanging her clothes, picks up the basin – now relieved of its weight – and disappears from the picture. The wind picks up. A gust comes from the north. A cloth (tablecloth, sheet, or tunic) is shaken, raised, and wrapped around the rope. There is something melancholy and then irreparable in that damp cloth, ever so slightly discoloured, victim of twisting and distortion. It seems impossible that it will ever be unknotted now. That from now on it will be like this: clinging to a rope in a suffocating embrace, strangling itself.

The young Sherpa rises and walks to his house.

Thirty-Nine

The body of the Englishman isn't totally alone: one of his trekking poles remains by his side. The other has hurtled away, irrecuperable. He's wearing his helmet, the ice axe sticking out from underneath his ribs. His rucksack is still strapped to his back, arching his dorsal vertebrae.

Perhaps the contemplation of that disheartening posture reminds the young Sherpa a little of something disquieting he has read online: as it turns out, Everest isn't necessarily the highest elevation on the planet. There is, say geologists, a divergence of criteria. The highest mountain in Nepal is, yes, the one that holds the record when measuring distance between summit and sea level. Those universally renowned 8,848 metres. But if, instead, with a different, more rigorous, less ground-hugging perspective the height were measured from the centre of the Earth, the giantess would lose her throne, be forced to abdicate in favour of the Andean magnificence of the Chimborazo volcano in the mountains of Ecuador. In other words: the South American peak, and not Everest, is the closest point on earth to outer space, to the celestial spheres, to Giordano Bruno's Renaissance dream. Because of the fact that the planet flattens at its poles and widens at the central parallel.

Even worse, the young Sherpa knows: not only is Everest not the undisputed highest peak on Earth, but also it is not – not by a long shot – the most difficult to climb. Annapurna, K2, Nanga Parbat present much more complex challenges in this same Himalayan range. Even more humiliating: the modest alpine heights of the Eiger and the Matterhorn are more feared by mountaineers than Everest.

Which is why, while looking at the Englishman splayed out on the rock, head cocked, helmet hiding his eyes, the young Sherpa says to himself: *International relations, why not? What would be the point in staying here?*

Error

"I want us to concentrate on Flavius' face when Pompey's name is mentioned. Where are Flavius' thoughts when Marullus recalls the Roman masses cheering Pompey so loudly that the Tiber 'trembled underneath her banks', as Shakespeare puts it? Most likely he thinks Pompey was a massive mistake. That anyone hailed by the plebs is the spawn of folly. How Sulla was a mistake before Pompey, and Cinna was a mistake before Sulla, and Gaius Marius before Cinna. And how Julius Caesar was an unmitigated error, the worst of all. The only unforgivable mistake. One that can only be repaired by way of a conspiracy and the most heinous of crimes."

Kan runu

Nima Chhiring was on the team of Sherpas hired by an expedition of Chinese mountaineers. On 18 April, he said goodbye to his boss and left Base Camp while it was still dark. He had decided to walk the three and a half kilometres to Camp One to make sure the path was in good enough condition to be climbed by his clients. On any given spring day, three and a half hours will suffice for a well-trained Sherpa to cover such a distance. Nima, with three summits under his belt, wore crampons on his boots and a backpack weighing around forty-five kilograms: his uniform. He walked, climbed slopes, went up aluminium ladders, hooked and unhooked his ropes dozens of times, all of it seeming routine. A few minutes after six in the morning, however, his trajectory was interrupted. In front of him, a traffic jam of Sherpas. Nearly a hundred of his colleagues stuck on a ledge of ice. They were smoking, chatting, some starting to feel the chill of early morning. Employed by different expeditions, they all had one identical mission: to verify the viability of the pathways of ascent and, if necessary, to prepare them. At this particular point, they had all encountered the same problem. A deep gap that yawned between two blocks of ice. The solution: tie two ladders together, secure them to the ledge, and point them to a lower level from where it would be possible to resume the ascent. When Nima arrived at the scene, most of the work had been done. Several Sherpas were already descending the ladders and preparing to resume their climb to Camp One. But all their movements were cautious, slow and frustrating. They dallied, feet suspended rung by aluminium rung, gazing at the ropes with excessive reverence, mistrusting the ice. Nima calculated that he'd have to wait at least half an hour for his turn to go down. He grew exasperated.

And in the midst of that exasperation, his ear started to cry. *Kan runu.* The mountain's warning. He began to panic. He tried to communicate with his leader at Base Camp. He wasn't there. He had gone all the way to Namche to purchase provisions. The expedition's cook answered the call. 'What's going on?' he asked. '*Kan runu.* I'm going back to base.' The Sherpas around him heard the conversation. '*Kan runu*? Are you sure?' they asked him. 'My ear is crying. I'm going down; all of you should go down, too,' he answered and began the descent. Seven Sherpas went with him: five out of respect for the crying ear; two because they were experiencing symptoms of frostbite on their feet. They made their way quickly. By a quarter to seven, they were already on an intermediate plain known as 'The Football Field'.

From that perspective, facing away from the summit, the phenomenology of an avalanche is registered like this: an abrupt gust, followed by a low, dry, deep noise. Fourteen thousand tons of ice; sixteen dead. All Sherpas.

Forty-Two

In spite of his galvanic temperament, it would be unusual for the old Sherpa to reproach his companion. He advises him, indoctrinates him, perhaps on occasion becomes a tad emphatic… but rarely does he rebuke him. That's because the older man has developed a theory about the Himalayan dialectic. A theory that is evidently wrong: Sherpas – the older man has convinced himself – take it for granted that, in the event of a disagreement, whoever is speaking must be right. The simple act of oration transforms the speaker into a bearer of truth. When the floor falls to another, rightness goes with it. But don't let this mislead you: few things are further from Nepalese idiosyncrasy than consensus. They never reach any agreement, the older man believes. What happens in an argument between Sherpas is nothing more and nothing less than an expansion of the experience of language.

But we ought not pay much attention to the old Sherpa's ideas. They tend to be confused, rebuttable. They tend towards mythologising. When he elaborates hypotheses standing on the southern slope of the giantess, the older man insists on not knowing that Sherpas argue like any other son of Cain. He ignores the numerous incidents of violence between Sherpas, how for centuries they have been shoved into the abyss over the slightest disagreements.

And the thing is that the old man, although he hates to admit it, is a foreigner: he was born very far from the Himalayas, on another continent. This has made him a fanatic of local folklore. Like the ex-smoker, like the convert, he, too, had to artificially invent his bona fides. He has done so by employing resistant materials.

By contrast, the Englishman who defencelessly occupies a contemptible portion of the mountain range was born in England. And his father, of course. And his grandfather, a child born in those years when almost everything was England.

Forty-Three

The young Sherpa tries to imagine his future as a career diplomat and immediately takes a step back: tight-fitting suits, cocktail parties, rented hypocrisy, the sterility of meetings, the insurmountable fence around the United Nations Security Council... Maybe not. Maybe diplomacy is not the best idea. After all, what is a country, a nation state? Or a nationality – what is that? Nobody knows any more. It happens all the time: pregnancies during wars and births that multiply over territories in conflict. Newborns poke out their heads just as the border has lost its definition. What flag flies over this forest? asks the new mother, the umbilical cord still warm beside the outcast placenta. The ambiguity of the sky responds to her with lazy generalities: some meteorological, others libertarian. But nationality is not resolved in abstractions, nor in instabilities. She must seek out another way to confer a homeland upon her infant child. How can this – all this – be fixed? There's no fixing it, the young Sherpa would say. But the old Sherpa wouldn't agree. There is only one way of solving it, he'd say: the production and exchange of documents. It is in bureaucracy, he would affirm, where *doxa* transforms into *episteme*.

Lady Houston

Lady Houston was the nickname of an eccentric British millionaire who had her moment of fame in the years leading up to World War II. On the one hand, she was a champion of women's rights and a promoter of women's suffrage; on the other, an ultra-nationalist and devoted benefactress of the empire's armaments. Her third husband was Sir Robert Houston, a conservative politician, member of Parliament and transoceanic trade magnate. It was said that when Sir Robert showed her his will, Lady Houston tore it to pieces and told him that bequeathing her only a million pounds was an insult to her integrity. From that afternoon forward, Sir Robert had his food professionally tasted in an effort to avoid being poisoned. He died, in any case, aboard a ship. And he left his wife five and a half million pounds.

But Lady Houston's arch nemesis wasn't her third husband, but rather Ramsay MacDonald, the first Labour man to make it to 10 Downing Street. In that building, Gandhi visited MacDonald in 1931 to start negotiations around the liberation of the political prisoners who had been arrested for demonstrating in favour of Indian independence. The image of the pacifist lawyer, barely clad in his dhoti robe and flip flops in front of the prime minister's residence, was an affront that Lady Houston could not bear. She immediately went on a campaign to establish a symbol of the supremacy of the United Kingdom over the colonies. She came up with the idea of setting up and financing the Houston-Mount Everest air expedition, the first flight over 'the mother of the world'. The mission was to be completed by two pilots commanding important aeroplanes: between the fuselages of both ships, the flag of Great Britain would fly at an altitude of more than 8,800 metres.

The flight had a successful outcome. The fact that this Himalayan region did not belong to rebellious India but to the pro-British Kingdom of Nepal struck Lady Houston as a minor detail. She sent a congratulatory telegram to the aviators: 'Your achievements have thrilled me through, oh brave men of my heart... If this does not make the Government sit up, nothing will... Sleep well and feel proud of yourselves, as we all are.' She then signed off with her usual '*Rule Britannia*'. Two years later, devastated by the abdication of Edward VIII, the wealthy Lady Houston decided not to eat any more and allowed herself to die.

The Young Sherpa

The only really vivid image, the only definite and accurate memory the young Sherpa has of his father is of the back of his neck. A nape with close-cropped hair that grew noticeably denser as it encroached upon the crown. A cubic nape, projecting at abrupt angles towards his temporal bones. Similar to the young Sherpa's own nape, just with more personality. As if the young Sherpa's skull had lost some definition through generational wear and tear.

That nape of his father's that the young Sherpa recalls was in an automobile. It must have been borrowed: the family never possessed any mode of transport of its own. Someone else's car, temporarily theirs, with no headrests, or central locking, or sound system. In the young Sherpa's anamnesis, it seems to have been some kind of holiday. Or a courtesy call to his grandparents in Kathmandu, meaning go, participate in some family ritual, and return in six to seven days. Walk five hours from Namche to Lukla, make use of the mail plane that charges bargain prices, land in the capital... Escape from the mountain. To the lowland, where spherical objects will roll in a manner more or less predictable, without flying out of control in their pursuit of a gravitational centre. Take, as well, the opportunity to see the area. Borrow a car, be – they, too, even Sherpas – tourists.

So his father had the steering wheel in his hands: a British steering wheel, situated on the right-hand side of the car, another inheritance of colonialism passed down to the Nepalese. He might have been driving with his elbow propped up on the frame of the open window, in which case the wind would have been blowing. But these are deductive reconstructions, spurious attempts; in the young Sherpa's memory, there is only a nape. And his mother, who was sitting in the front seat on the left, a cloth bag on her lap; and in the back, his sister and the young Sherpa himself, his perspective, their seatbelts without inertial locking mechanisms, fastened at the level of their armpits.

At the start of this sequence, it was not yet night, although a vector into darkness could already be perceived. They must have been returning to Kathmandu. His sister was complaining about something in an irritated tone, but soon she was asleep, her head bouncing oneiric off the window. His mother was silent, upholding the status quo through sheer concentration. The young Sherpa's eyes were open and on the back of his father's neck as his father's physiognomy changed according to the colour progression of dusk. Frank afternoon led first to an ephemeral evening fading; then, to the throes of the arc of twilight; finally, now, a night that was timid and clear; the estuary that extended into the dense starry vault; the weight of that threat.

The young Sherpa was distracted for a moment by what was outside their borrowed car, and he tried to divine shapes in that nocturnal clarity: rocks, here and there a sign of human occupation, an abandoned home, the remains of a dead animal near the road's shoulder.

In the intermittent velocity of the road through the foothills, a static moon followed the car's path without distraction. Everything was moving, everything left behind except the moon that remained anchored in the sky and, at the same time, in perpetual motion, imitating, perhaps becoming the guardian of, the young Sherpa's family journey. So he – three years old, his ignorance astronomical – looked at the moon and wondered why it was chasing them, what they had done to it. How it managed to be in the same place always, yet all the time with them. He looked at the back of his father's neck, shaved so close, pale in the selenite light. Then he went back to the moon: why was it so hard to leave behind?

The Snow Is the Postcard

It is the old Sherpa's belief that snow makes the mountain ugly. And grass, too, and any type of vegetation. Any living organism, really. But above all: snow. The old Sherpa would prefer for the mountain to be the mass accumulation of raw bare rock, exhibiting only the traces of erosion. Without grandiloquence. An alliance of chromatically similar minerals: a series of rocks that would paint upon the mountain's slopes a gamut of greys and browns, ochre, tan, charcoal smidges sliding into the whitish ignominy of curdled milk. A stone that would look like the skin of a young rhinoceros alongside another that would recall the sun setting over a dromedary's hump. And so on, from foot to summit, one rock after the next. Seen from a distance, a magnificent spectacle – struggle of fragments to achieve a single collective identity, one dun that would define, that would allow for nomenclature. Up close, the marvel of detail, of nuance, of difference.

And yet, thinks the old Sherpa, *the snow is the postcard*. When a tourist imagines the summit of Everest, the first thing that comes to mind is snow. The uniform snow, at once coarse and pretentious. With its infinite configurations applied to the futility of the flake. No two are alike, marvel simple minds. There's no such thing as identical, the old Sherpa would like to respond. What we say of snowflakes could apply equally well to the waves in the ocean, the grains of sand in the desert, the bottles produced on a factory belt in Detroit. No two are the same... And the sky? one might inquire. Isn't the sky always one in its variegation? Is it not the same blue, even when it's cloudy, even at night? No, the old Sherpa would say: No. It's not the same, and it's not anything. We can't pretend the sky is anything as though there were an above, or the aspiration to be culminated, or a below, or an ahead. As though nature were not an aberrant uninter-rupted concatenation of states of matter and energy, or, in even more perfidious cases, a random continuity of consciousness. And yet, in spite of everything, the snow stays unchanging on the postcard.

For the seasoned climber, on the other hand, the summit of Mount Everest is silence. If the maddening roar of the wind roving over the top of the highest peak on Earth can be considered silence.

Forty-Seven

"**S**hakespeare never clarifies what type of tribune Flavius might be. He might be a *military tribune*; that is to say, an official embittered over a loss of power in the hierarchical structure of Rome. Messenger from the central government in the midst of the legions, his position would have been weakened by an imperial leadership arising over every segment of the machinery of war. Julius Caesar's leadership, of course. This had become an ideal position for children of patrician families without a lot going for them but who wanted a place in the State. I am inclined to think that Flavius was not one of those. I think he was more likely a *tribune of the plebs*. That is, a representative of the people before the Senate. The position of tribune of the plebs was created by popular pressure: a way of seating a commoner in the capital of the empire. An ordinary man invested with a political position conferred by the delegation of territorial sovereignty. To every tribe, a tribune elected by franchise. Flavius strikes me as one of those.

"His reaction, however, is completely alien to the feelings of the Roman people. He rebukes the citizens, censures their joy, lectures them. He nods as his companion Marullus qualifies those who celebrate the arrival of Julius Caesar: 'You blocks, you stones, you worse than senseless things!' He assents when Marullus blurts: 'O you hard hearts, you cruel men of Rome.'

"So what is it this play is trying to tell us in its very first scene? It doesn't matter. The author is Shakespeare, and he, like Isaac Newton, does not formulate hypotheses: he limits himself to describing the psychic mechanisms of man. That is something to keep in mind when the curtains open and you, young actor, must speak your line: 'Hence! Home, you idle creatures, get you home!'"

Forty-Eight

The old Sherpa attempts to reconstruct the moment of the fall. As if surrounding the episode with a story might serve as a shortcut to establish how much time has passed since then. He recalls that everything was relatively silent. The Englishman was walking between them; the young Sherpa was bringing up the rear. They had come to a curve. To the left, the slope; to the right, the void. It wasn't complicated. It was practically a passageway, an asphalted street. They could have pitched a tent there, even, spent the night. It wasn't an upward stretch. The old Sherpa underscores this idea: it wasn't upward. It was completely horizontal, posing not the slightest risk. *That's why we didn't have the ropes attached to the harnesses, that's why we were walking free, each according to his abilities and each according to his needs*, he thinks. Once they were around the bend, but only then – then yes, they would arrive at a period of clambering, of having to best the verticality of the mountain. But not yet. *But for now it was an avenue, a polystyrene highway, a yielding plaza.*

It might not have been ten minutes, even. Six since it happened; eight, at the most. The old Sherpa leading the charge. He heard a *tsk*, a tongue pulling away from a set of teeth. Annoyance. That was what that *tsk* expressed. Not fear, not surprise, not the unstoppable anger of mortals in the face of their finitude. None of that. Annoyance: like a father on discovering that the laces of his child's shoes have come undone. Like someone who observes, after washing and drying the dishes, that the pan is still dirty on the stove, greasy, unpostponable. The old Sherpa heard that *tsk* and turned his head. He saw that the Englishman was stumbling, moving his arms like rattan blades, wanting to regain his balance.

A mistake. The best option, always, is to fall.

Dragonfly

Or that other morning, in the classroom. The young Sherpa remembers it vividly. It was a very short-lived class, in which their teacher briefly tried to instruct them on the differences between domestic and wild animals, between mammals and amphibians, between being brave and being heedless. Does the old Sherpa have this kind of memory? Evocations of this sharpness?

That day, the young Sherpa, who was almost ten years old now, entered the school building, walked – feet of an automaton – into the classroom, sat, and waited. He was in the first row, his backpack by his side. Behind him, tumult, that juvenile mob, those slumping desks, the projection of a centre aisle, floor of heavy tiles in perspective. Their teacher arrived, prompting a simulacrum of silence: no one stopped talking, but now their chats, their imprecations, their snorts were all muffled. Their teacher greeted them; she was nice, but possibly only because she knew no other variants of character. She conveyed warmth by virtue of exclusion. She looked around the room, asked if anyone was absent, turned to face the blackboard and wrote: 'mammals', 'reptiles', 'birds', 'fish', 'amphibians'. The order was random, but then, what can one expect from a taxonomy?

Her students surrendered themselves to the machinery of morning somnolence. They listened from afar, distracted by very remote stimuli, some noting down individual words, most pondering life outside: the morning, the sun, the possibility of pushing one another. And, in the midst of that torpor, the call of chaos.

'A dragonfly!' a child sounded the alarm. 'Where?' 'Here, inside, here!' Instantly the atmosphere got choppy. The whole school day took a turn. Adrenaline and anomie. The insect bouncing off the classroom window. Bumping its head against the pane and plummeting in confusion. Flapping its little elliptical wings and lunging once more at that transparency. Screams. Not always directly linked to the insect, but always derived from its presence.

The young Sherpa – pure thoughtless instinct – felt called. He got up and faced the aisle with no one's consent or permission. He stalked between his peers, their voices overlapping on account of that joyous advent of disorder. The dragonfly, megacephalic, was performing, in that moment, a manoeuvre of ascension. Gathering momentum, trying to locate a gap between the pane and the window frame. It would fail, it wouldn't give up, and it would try again. The young Sherpa reached the spot and regarded the dragonfly. Took stock of it. He leaped and was standing with both feet atop a chair, half crushing a classmate, and in that equilibrium, in that instability, he achieved the feat: one swift motion, and he had seized the insect by its tail.

He exhibited it right away. The bug twisted in between his massive fingers. The young Sherpa felt a hint of apprehension at that vital viscosity, which in any case had no chance of competing with the prehensile pride of his phalanxes. Around him rose applause, but there was also a hint of disappointment to the group dynamic now. The certainty that the singularity had entered its declining phase. That the brief anarchic hubbub the dragonfly had introduced into the boredom and frustration of the classroom was already in its death throes. Midway between vanity and pathos, the young Sherpa promenaded through the classroom with the dragonfly between his fingers and his eyes fixed on the blackboard. The boys renewed their curiosity and asked to pet the insect, kill it, put it in the mouths of their companions. Someone said:

'It's disgusting – why don't you toss it out?'

The young Sherpa nodded but continued his parade, his triumph down the aisle; haughty but with a touch of unease at the imploring buzz of the insect between his fingers. Another voice begged him:

'Don't kill it.'

This pious invocation swayed the young Sherpa. And so he shook his head, went back to the window, opened it with his other hand and hurled the dragonfly into the outside world.

The teacher, meanwhile, was struggling with a piece of chalk. She was trying to draw gills on the summary corpus of a fish unveiled in profile to general indifference. In the wake of that gregarious overflow, all the children were continuing to watch the young Sherpa, even now that there was no longer anything to see. In reality, the dragonfly episode had maxed out his capacity for being witnessed. As a child, the young Sherpa didn't know what to do with all those eyes on him. Would he prefer for them to ignore him, then? Not quite. The best thing, he thought at that moment, would be to be able to look at them without them realising. No. The ideal, the extraordinary thing would be for them to watch him all the time, and for him not to even notice. For no one to be able to take their eyes off him.

Zenithal

If the view were zenithal, distant, the landscape would be very different. Three men: two standing, one lying in a strange position, pointing west. There is a constituent immobility to the whole of the picture. The one lying down, we'd presume from up here, is the one who feels most comfortable with the current state of affairs. The two men who are vertical, on the other hand, transmit a certain tension, a degree of discomfort that needs for its resolution not a kinetic escape, but rather something more elusive, some sort of electricity, of static to surround them.

Of course, as soon as we move away a little, the detail loses definition. And in particular it loses interest, drama. Taking this distance, the three figures on the mountainside are no more important than that goat or that heap of tents, thousands of metres behind them, where six Spaniards, one Frenchwoman, and five other Sherpas are camped. From this height, the organic is relegated to the background to make way for the panorama. It is not yet a planetary dimension, we have not gone far enough to ponder the sphericity of the Earth, its bluish patina, the cosmic immensity… Not yet. It's more like the height of a helicopter, of an audacious condor, of a water bomber plane that rises with its cargo already unleashed upon the flames of the forest. From this height, neither exaggerated nor close, the perspective rearranges priorities. The important thing from here seems to be the snow. And to a lesser extent the rock. Impossible to see the sky from up here, looking down. Some of the flora really strive to be part of the picture. As for the fauna, they are just stains, annoyances that spoil the general composition, the continuity of the white. The three immobile figures are part of that fauna. Pieces of a food chain with no role assigned.

Now one of them moves. From here it is difficult to say for certain, but it would appear that one of them has moved. He disrupts the diorama. They are adorable when they move, from this height. With their little arms, their tiny wool caps. There he goes, yes, he's moving. He lifts his eyes to the sky and looks.

Fifty-One

Where did he come from, though? What combination of mishaps and luck swept the old Sherpa up the southern slope of Mount Everest? The young Sherpa encounters no answer, though this doesn't upset him. Not at all. Rather, it remains dissolved in his consciousness, where other anxieties float in a reverie of frosted panes.

He looks at the sky, the snow-capped peaks, and without saying anything lets his gaze get lost over imprecisions in the landscape. An ache, a faint helplessness afflicts him; this happens every time he goes away from Namche, his home, its habitual slopes and its tourists and that flow of foreign exchange... Or perhaps it's something else. The truth is that there is something in the inactivity of waiting that ushers the young Sherpa into a phantasmagoric zone. A place that is not the resinous chaos of the present, but also not the fossil past. A site that has no form. It's hard to give it a name. The magmatic, perhaps. Something that at first manifests itself as a devastated region of snippets of unfinished information: the damp on the low walls of his house, the door of a piece of furniture that came off its hinges and must be fastened with a piece of cardboard, the pictures of his father...

the starrily ragged reverberation of the physical presence of that father, which has already started to harden, to set as a memory of memories. Which is already getting distanced in the evanescence of anecdotes recounted in third person.

'The forklift fell over with your dad and three other people inside.'

His mother's explanation never went beyond that. That was all that could be said. But for the young Sherpa, by some quirk of the economy of grief, it was impossible to picture the scene: the going wrong, a forklift falling just because, that sudden imprisoning, the influence of budget on the wear and tear of the equipment.

It seemed to work better for him, as the years went by, to convert the fall of the forklift into a car wreck. Something similar, but less involuntary; with a slight dose of the epic came a minimal responsibility for one's own demise. He constructed his personal accident rate with a specific point of view: partly obscured by the nape of his father, who was driving the car, and the other three dead people who would squeeze in beside him in the back seat so as to all be in the frame at the very moment of the fall. At sunset, with a sun that was already setting but still gleaming against the snow-capped peaks of the Himalayas. And then the landscape and its Expressionist acceleration out the window. The impact.

Fifty-Two

In 1938, the gaze that lingers over the Himalayas does not originate in England, but rather within the edifices of central Berlin. The Society for Research and Teaching on German Ancestral Heritage, known more familiarly as the Ahnenerbe, dispatches a team of naturalists, functionaries of the Reich, and occult enthusiasts. The mastermind behind the expedition is Heinrich Himmler. The objective of their voyage isn't entirely clear. There are negotiations between Nazi functionaries and Tibetan leaders: there is talk of arms, of Chinese power, of the influence of Great Britain in the region. There are also anthropometric records that seek to establish a link between Aryan genealogy and the ethnicity of the locale. An esoteric investigation into the Yeti is launched. Some three hundred animal skins are collected. One hundred and eight ancient volumes of the Buddhist canon are confiscated. It is all kept in absolute secret.

The expedition returns to Germany in August, 1939. On the 1st of September, Hitler invades Poland.

Out of Sight

The young Sherpa's mind was elsewhere. His angle of sight kept him shut out of the moment. The curve precluded action. The old Sherpa would speak of the advantages of the oscillatory. He'd say you have to make turns slowly, not letting yourself be overtaken by vertigo. He'd say you have to enjoy the detour, even at the risk of procrastination. The young Sherpa wouldn't be so sure. He wouldn't care so much whether the path is straight or crooked, more its orography. Is the path flat? Is it downhill? Is there a lot of scree? The young Sherpa was bringing up the rear, watching the Englishman's back. But the event occurred on a bend. First the older man rounded it, and then the tourist. The young Sherpa lost sight of them. It was a moment, if *moment* means anything. First he observed, from the side, the old Sherpa disappearing behind a rock. Then he saw the Englishman exiting the frame. Once he was – you might say – alone, the younger man lowered his eyes to analyse the precise point on the mountain where he was about to rest his right foot. It could have been – what? – three seconds the young Sherpa took to take that step, and then four more with a half twist of the shoulder girdle, and in the end, to make his way around the curve: no longer looking south, but northeast. And it was in those three seconds that the young Sherpa would come to understand the dramatic potential of the out-of-sight.

There is a well-founded idea born in Mitteleuropa and perfected in France: everything we've grown accustomed to calling *life* is, in reality, a *symptom*. Actions, thoughts, interpretations, dialogues and soliloquies, sufferings… are nothing more than intermittently surging projections, stamps on the surface of the knowable. *Symptoms*. The real is in the out-of-sight, permeating from an aberrant beyond. It's inaccessible. And yet we keep conforming to the merely perceptible. Somewhat like the way astronomers infer the presence of an invisible black hole by means of its gravitational effects. The real is missing: we can only begin to glimpse its consequences.

His eyes aimed northeast now, the young Sherpa became aware of the Englishman's absence. Then, in a flash that was similar to simultaneity, he saw the older man, who had already crawled towards the edge. And right away he made himself believe: *He didn't kill him.*

Fifty-Four

The old Sherpa twists his neck and looks for an instant behind him. Their things are propped up against the slope: the logistical paraphernalia of mountaineering. Backpacks, ice axes, harnesses, ropes, ladders, tents, tin bowls, crampons for their boots... All of it in vain, as it's turned out. Worse: grotesque.

But

The Englishman didn't want to fall. The Englishman wanted to stay standing. Like a vegetable. Which is why the old Sherpa saw him stagger like an ostrich on mescaline, open his eyes, cross his right foot leftward, try to find a foothold, wave his arms. All useless: the best thing is to fall, thought the old Sherpa as he observed the changes of expression in the gestures of the Englishman. From disgruntlement to panic in three simple stages. The intermediate stage, imperceptible, faster than fleeting, is the one that's most ridiculous. Disgruntlement, ridiculousness, panic. In that order. First, a *tsk*: disgruntlement. Then, a word: the ridiculousness of orality. What word? What did the Englishman say before falling into the brief chasm of eight, nine metres to the ledge? 'But', he said. He wanted to make his case. I'm stumbling, 'but'. Yes, I'm losing my balance, 'but'. All right, all right, I'm tumbling over now, 'but'. Then, panic.

Fifty-Six

The young Sherpa was going inside his house, he remembers now. He took off his shoes, left his backpack next to an armchair, gave his mother a kiss; his sister hadn't come back yet. He remembers now. Does the old Sherpa remember similar images? Does he have a clarified past he can return to in moments of nostalgia or misgivings? The young Sherpa does. He reaffirms this as he leans over the edge: he went inside; he took off his shoes. He left his backpack next to the chair. He lingered in front of a photo, his mother's favourite. The young Sherpa was only a few months old in the picture, and his father was laughing, holding him up. His older sister, in the background, was concentrating on looking at her hands. All of them were wearing their coats: it was in Namche, at home, the same home where the photo is displayed. But you couldn't see the landscape. Their windows were closed. His mother interrupted his contemplation of the image. She asked him questions from the kitchen, and he responded:

'Good.'

He didn't say anything about his father.

'You know, the usual.'

Nor the memory of his father.

'No, they didn't give us anything.'

From the kitchen came, too, the smell of a still-distant dinner. The young Sherpa – eleven years old, indolent – found this part of the day fatiguing. He didn't have anything left to do. He stood in front of the TV, which was on. He reached for the remote control, repaired with duct tape so the batteries wouldn't fall out, and he began to flip around. From channel to channel, the appeal was in the linkage of images, in the production of meaning through contiguity. But his mother was less amenable to that Soviet filmic feeling: she peeked in from the kitchen, her apron eroded by white soap. She announced that it would be a while still before dinner, and that they were going to have to wait for his sister. With a gesture, a mute overturning of the palm of her hand, she demanded he surrender the remote. First she put on the news: a plane crash, victims and relatives of victims, and specialists in black boxes, downcast lashes and lapel mics, animated infographics. A hundred and seven dead. The skeleton of the plane, the jungle surrounds, the shot from a helicopter, and the secret, morbid expectation that it, too, would plummet, would contribute five or six more cadavers to the chyron. His mother grew weary, changed it: a fashion channel, a show of lingerie, electronic music, strobe lights. The young Sherpa – eleven years old, healthy Oedipal transmigration – was captivated by these images. His mother went into the kitchen to check on something in her saucepans. He stayed staring at the screen. He could have spent hours looking at those girls (mature or prepubescent, exploited or overpaid) strutting down the catwalk, and whenever one of them turned to leave, another would appear, identical and completely different. This one's nipples could be seen through her bra, and the young Sherpa put his right hand to one eyebrow and

128

pressed, trying to keep something inside his skull that was struggling to get out. He wouldn't have liked his mother to see him watching those girls on TV, but he couldn't change the channel. His only recourse was to flee. Into the kitchen.

He found his mother stirring a pot with a wooden spoon that was split at the end. He, too, felt like dipping a spoon into the food. To try it, since he was really getting hungry now. But there wasn't another spoon. So he just stood there. Contemplating the concentric circles that his mother traced over the stew, respecting the circumference of the pot. And he remembered his father. But otherwise, differently. He attained that point where ideas fold their edges and take on a whole new nature: capable of being thought in themselves. The young Sherpa – eleven years old, a martyr – could already bask in his fatherless anguish, even then. He left the kitchen and went back to where the photo was. He took another look at the image of his father lifting him and understood that he could now do without everything previously registered as real, without the old searing. That was because there was something special about desperation, he realised. It was warm, hospitable. Then he thought about himself, or about what was happening to him, and he found that that temperature and that salinity, which had previously made him want to cry, were now a thermal bath, a pool he could just surrender to. The sulphurous steam made everything ambiguous, the responsibility to the world was vaguer now. The image of his father merely an excuse to plunge his chin into the healing waters of a longing without bearings.

Fifty-Seven

With the Second World War over, twenty years after the flight financed by Lady Houston over the summit of Everest, and as nineteenth-century colonialism gives way to new forms of imperial intervention, England maintains its anachronistic obsession with incorporating the planet's highest peak into its showcase. The Crown entrusts the mission to John Hunt, Baron of Llanfair Waterdine and an officer in His Majesty's army. Hunt takes the job seriously: he recruits top-notch mountaineers from across the Commonwealth and sets off for Nepal. He reaches Kathmandu with his team, and they install themselves at the embassy of the United Kingdom, where Hunt will plan the expedition. The next day he hires a group of Sherpas. When night falls, the mountaineers retire to their rooms. The Sherpas ask Hunt about their rooms. The British nobleman replies that there aren't any beds for them. That the appropriate thing for the Sherpas is to sleep on the floor, like they do on the mountain. In protest, at dawn the next day, the group of Sherpas goes out to urinate on the sidewalk before breakfast.

Fifty-Eight

'These people...'

The old Sherpa is speaking. He sees that the younger man nods but says nothing. Does the young man's silence signify assent? the older man wonders. And sinks back into his drifting mind.

On the one hand, a reproduction of Turner, the Tibetan songs, the polished parquet of a spacious apartment in Amsterdam, or Zurich. Almost all of what's wrong with this world. *'Porters', they call us when they're there, these people.* What people? These people: the people who visit the mountain. *These people: self-indulgent visitors*, thinks the old Sherpa. Those who see themselves as 'mountaineers', or 'climbers'. A few, aware of their limitations, add a direct modifier, something adjectival, that limits their scope: 'amateur mountaineer', for example. Or 'fledgling mountaineer'. But for the Sherpas, anyone who comes to the mountain with the intention of ascending is a visitor, plain and simple, an undesirable. A tourist. That much can be taken for granted. *We are Sherpas; they are tourists.*

Fifty-Nine

Fourteen thousand tons of snow and ice. Sixteen dead. Three days after the avalanche and the *kan runu* of Nima Chhiring, the Sherpas called on the Nepalese authorities to suspend all ascents of Everest for the remainder of the season. From Kathmandu, the government declined the request. Instead, officials offered the bereaved financial compensation. Five thousand six hundred dollars to be distributed among the sixteen families: three hundred and fifty dollars for each one.

Sixty

On the other hand, if the young Sherpa were asked, if someone came up to him, tapped him on the shoulder and dragged him by force from his ideas regarding naval engineering and the foreign service, he would have a somewhat different vision. With a different focus. The young Sherpa would say that he sees himself as the agent of a transaction. A subject with a certain kind of knowledge, to whom laypeople turn in search of advice. An expert who possesses a certain set of skills the layperson lacks. Like a mechanic or a dentist? No. More like a teacher, someone overseeing a graduate thesis, or like a prostitute with particular expertise in sexual propaedeutics. From this perspective, the young Sherpa would say, an exchange takes place here: money for learning. You could even take it one step further and raise the analogy to religious heights. The Sherpas would be the illuminated, those chosen for their understanding, and it is their duty to show the way to the uninitiated, teach the process of ascesis, of unveiling. In this sense, the young Sherpa would argue, the monetary covenant is simply an imposition in the circulation of gifts. In order to accomplish the ascent, the tourist has to pay, not to fulfil a commercial requirement, but rather as penitence, as loss: the price of attaining understanding. If the tourist pays, it is because that pecuniary release is what sets him on the path to revelation.

Summit

On May 29, 1953, John Hunt's expedition finally reaches the summit of Mount Everest. The Baron of Llanfair Waterdine does not accomplish this feat in person. It is two other members of his team who plant the flag of the United Kingdom at the peak. Neither of them was born on the British Isles. One is a New Zealander: Edmund Hillary; the other, a Sherpa: Tenzing Norgay. The news takes four days to reach London, where it competes on the front pages of the papers with the coronation of Elizabeth II as Queen of the United Kingdom and Northern Ireland and of Her Other Realms and Territories, Head of the Commonwealth, Defender of the Faith.

Sixty-Two

If the old Sherpa were to hear the hypothetical soliloquy of his partner, he would not remain silent. He would insist that the commercial equation that arises between tourist and Sherpa is riddled with asymmetries. He would suggest that the tourist, no matter how sizeable the fortune he pays, does so through a prism that condemns the Sherpas to objectification. The old Sherpa sees himself more as an artefact. In terms of classical economics, the Sherpa is neither demand nor supply, but rather merchandise, tradable goods; capital, at most. We are tractors, the old Sherpa would say. Machines capable of performing human tasks better and faster. Worse still, he'd say: we are machines predating the Industrial Revolution. We are animals. The tourists reduce us to animality.

And then the old Sherpa would recommend to his young colleague that he linger for a moment on the faces of the tourists when they return from the top of the mountain. He'd recommend – he who has seen them up there above it all – that the Young Sherpa remember that moment, when the foreigners realise that they have emerged victorious over the improbable ascent and can now exert their dominance over the globe from a height of 8,848 metres. Because it is then, he would explain to him, that the tourists become convinced that they have proven their heroism. The foreigners who reach the summit believe that they have outperformed the species and, at least for an instant, they see themselves as demigods. They celebrate, they hug, they take pictures (because they always take pictures, always relapse into narcissism, always take phenomenology down to the level of the souvenir).

Meanwhile, the Sherpas wait to one side, not making much of a distinction between ascent and descent; just silently grateful that none of these bumpkins broke a leg during the expedition. For them, for the tourists, we are pack animals, the older man would say. Creatures capable of doing with relative ease what for human beings constitutes a feat. They see us as mules, beings with bone structures suited to lugging great weights. They see it as perfectly logical for Sherpas to summit. They ought to think of us as Titans, deities with powers unattainable by mere mortals. But they don't. When they reach the summit, they're the ones who are the heroes. It is they who have achieved mountaineering glory, the – so-called – miracle of besting, of overcoming themselves. The fact that the Sherpa has undertaken the same labour not once, but three times, five times, ten times seems natural to the tourist, in the same way that it seems natural, unmeritorious that an elephant should be able to tear up a tree by its roots.

In actual fact, however, no one asks the older Sherpa his opinion, no one taps his shoulder to pose any question. In fact, these arguments are still barely lucubration, an introspective murmur that swills and develops until a jovial voice interrupts:

'Shall we get up?'

The Pledge

The last photograph of his father. Taken a few months before the forklift crash. An enlargement has been pasted onto a mat and displayed on the wall. The whole family is in it. All huddled in an insignificant central portion of the frame, as though afraid of not fitting. In one of the upper sections of the image, a cloud casts its shadow over a portion of the grass, not where the family is, but rather significantly farther back. Standing, wearing a light-coloured tunic, the mother holds in her arms her younger child, who is gazing with avid eyes at something that is beyond the camera lens. The mother is indicating to the young Sherpa the thing that captures the attention of both of them, but which neither could recall today. Below, directly below, the father is squatting with his mouth slightly ajar, as though in the middle of a sentence. His forearms on his thighs and his gaze tilted leftward, where the young Sherpa's older sister, just turned six, is staring at the floor.

'A beetle,' his sister will respond even today if asked what she was subjecting to such scrutiny back then.

In none of the photos displayed in the young Sherpa's house can the mountain be seen. Nor the Caterpillar that his father used for over a decade to remove, by municipal order, the snow from the streets of Namche. The engine of that Caterpillar, the sound of that familiar, mournful engine, returns to the young Sherpa's auditory memory now, on the mountain, as he wonders: does the older man have a source, a course, a delta? Or is he like an ocean that merely varies its height according to the caprices of the moon? He knows that he himself does have an origin, a dossier. Milestones and key dates.

The day of the pledge of allegiance to the flag of Nepal, for example. The young Sherpa – aged ten, neither anxiety nor melancholy, but rather the tedium of transitoriness – as he walks to school. Almost no breakfast: first the tea was too hot, and then it was undrinkable. Now he feels as if he might be hungry; this is corroborated by a ventral rumble, acid secretions causing his internal organs to quake. He goes inside; he hardly responds to the greetings of his classmates, nor the shoving, nor the bad words that have now come back into fashion; it must have been three years since he last heard so many profanities at school.

Suddenly everyone else leaves. The twelve-year-olds, the seven-year-olds, the eight-year-olds. They all go into their classrooms. But not the ten-year-olds: they stay. The pledge is about to begin. Just like that, without preamble. The young Sherpa follows the line, dragging his feet.

Atop a pole, the flag of Nepal. The only national flag in the world that isn't rectangular. A source of pride, a proclamation, an extravagant thing with two overlapping triangles, red geometry with bright blues and dynastic symbols. Pure visual ecumenism to unite, under one and the same State, Hindus and Buddhists. There is that oddity, that dysphoria on the event horizon. It functions all the same. It can be hoisted, and it even waves a little if there's wind enough; it does not cease to be a flag. And it can be drawn, which makes the young Sherpa's life easier. Not like the emblem of Nepal, and its irreproducible motif: Everest surrounded by red rhododendrons and the silhouette of domestic territory, with its absolutely white outline, to the point that it looks more like a snowfall, an avalanche about to fall on the two hands, a woman's and a man's, that shake without any sensuality. Below the emblem, the motto of Nepal engraved in Sanskrit: 'The mother and the fatherland are greater than the Kingdom of Heaven.' Exalted nationalism and Oedipus proclaiming – at the top of his lungs – his measureless love for Jocasta.

The pledge ceremony takes place without the young Sherpa even noticing. There is, of course, a nationalist mantra that he whispers, looking down. There is also an entourage: classmates, faculty, parents, photographs that will wind up in online traffic, slander… the democracy of jouissance. He doesn't want to see that. He prefers the automatism of reciting what he's learned, emptying it of meaning; locking his eyes on the tips of his boots.

But at some point he's going to have to look at something other than the ground again. Ahead, to either side. Up, at least: the two red triangles flapping in the east wind, the mountain range behind, the cloudless sky. And in none of these places will he find his mother, who is already attending to the tourists at the Namche Tourist Service desk. Nor his father, sole inhabitant of the Kingdom of the Skies, that Nepalese *topos hyperuranios*, a Platonic studio apartment smaller than a mother and a fatherland, but in any case, inaccessible. Is that right? Did the forklift fall all the way up there?

Sixty-Four

W ho was the Englishman arguing with before losing his footing and falling some ten metres into the void, neither on his back, nor on his face, but rather sort of on his side, like those Hollywood swimmers thrown one by one into a pool, smiling, looking into the camera lens, animating a truncated choreography that can only be expanded in the editing room? Who did the Englishman say 'but' to at the last moment he felt he could keep his balance? Who was the intended recipient of the astringent echo of those three Anglo-Saxon letters pronounced without stridency, in a low voice, as though part of an intimate, a murmured dialogue?

The old Sherpa, the sole auditory witness to that last foreign word, tends to think that it was a transcendental message, a supplication, a plea arising from the sudden despair of a man who is falling. But it could also have been an internal conversation. An intracorporeal message: a leg that speaks to a shoulder, or a subcutaneous organ, let's assume enzymatic, that suddenly realises the entire system is under threat and presents its complaint to the Central Committee: 'But…'

Why the Mountain?

Why the mountain? Why not the steppe or the wetlands? What attracted the old Sherpa to the mountain range, given that he, born far from everything, could have chosen the tropics or the tundra? Something must have summoned him from the high mountains. Possibly the obscene concentration of rocks, more than the snow. The hardness more than the altitude. The mass more than the atmospheric intimacy. That and the fact he wanted to get away from the sea.

The old Sherpa lived in a city. Avenues and pedestrian streets, out-of-control morbidity and scant urban planning. The old Sherpa lived a peaceful life in that metropolis with its immodest accident rates and unequal distribution of the surplus. He had a degree from a university, a routine: work, consumption, rest, diversions. He had flat-rate internet. His parents were understanding; his friends were friendly. He lived alone. Comfortable. He wasn't poor, nor was he very sick. He didn't belong to a cult, didn't believe in all conspiracy theories, nor was he permanently numbed. Of course: the old Sherpa was young.

He decided to go on vacation one day. To the coast, a seaside peninsula, he sought the sun, the sea. Even he doesn't know why. He bought his ticket, packed his suitcase, got on the bus with its soft seats. He arrived, some — a few — days passed, he met Rabbit, met Rabbit's husband, heard about the war. He decided to go far away. He became a world-weary flâneur. A few years later he settled down. And for this purpose, the old Sherpa chose the Himalayas.

The first days on the coast were perfect and disappointing. Sun, beach, sea, another routine: the idyllic tableau and its ellipsis above the salty residue in the groin, sand on the scalp, and sunstroke. It was waking up and having a dream breakfast: caffeine and starchy foods imposing the inertia of habit on the supply of fruits and cereals, dairy products, eggs and cold cuts. The hotel, its buffet, its pomp.

Not until he had got his money's worth for that fourth of what the bed and breakfast cost did he retire to his bedroom once more. A premature siesta: he'd sleep from noon to three in the afternoon. Half past three. Four o'clock at the latest. Then he would change and go to the beaches of the peninsula. He tried not to go back to the same one. Every day a new landscape. Similar, risibly similar. But new. What never changed was his equipment: just a towel, sunglasses in their case (to keep his money in), flip-flops, a t-shirt, a bathing suit, a book.

Fifteen metres from the shore, he would stretch out on the sand. He'd read lying on his back. Holding the book in such a way that its shadow prevented him from being blinded by the sun. Alternating arms, of course. Two pages with the left; three with the right. He'd read for half an hour, forty minutes. Then he'd turn over. He'd take off his t-shirt, improvise a pillow. He was still capable of dozing some fifteen minutes more. He'd wake up and go into the water. Not for long. A little while: what it took him to realise his surroundings left him indifferent, when they weren't outright disagreeable. The children and their shrieks, their egotism; those adult men and their feigned nonchalance, that laid-back alienation of the summer season; the elderly and imminence. Not much longer. The same waves pushed the old Sherpa out of the sea, and he walked back to his towel, his flip-flops, feeling layers of protection, all of them justified and all of them false: isolation, exceptionality, self-pity… The fatty tissue of consciousness.

And so on, for how long? Three, four days? A different beach each time. Sleep, have breakfast, sleep, beach, read, sleep, sea, sleep… Dinner? Barely: it didn't take much for the old Sherpa to get by. So he would grab something light at the corner store, and that would be his meal. A yogurt. Low-fat. Or less. Sleep, beach, sleep, sea, sleep, yogurt, read, sleep, breakfast, sleep… And so on, for how long? Three, four days when the old Sherpa felt safe? How long until the women showed up?

Denial, solitude. On the fifth or fourth day, it occurred to the old Sherpa to look at the women on the beach: pre-teens, teens, college girls, new mums, seasoned mums, leathery old ladies who held his gaze a few seconds before sinking into the surf. Women walking right up to sunset along the beaches of the peninsula. The old Sherpa was young: onanism, angst. The moment when the surface of the frozen lake fissures, that burst.

Because once the women passed by, just before sunset, on the sand, the children were no longer shouting their rambunctious shouts, prisoners of the most ill-tempered caprices, but were instead quite fragile, and you had to bite your knuckles to resist the urge to race to their sides, to sit down in the dunes, hug them and keep them away from the currents, from the currents' scaly monsters, their depths, the abysmal dark, the giant squids and their tentacular forces that would snatch away all they had of any importance, all of their potential. Once the women passed and held his gaze a few seconds before plunging into the foam of the summer swell, the adults no longer looked falsely disinterested, but rather fraternal in their despair, victims, too, of that grinding clash of gears, companions in perdition, people to hand off the oars of Charon's boat to. This is what the women who passed by and allowed themselves to be looked at brought, these women who held his gaze for several seconds: a new sense of belonging, a solitary impulse that was impossible to say no to, one that transformed the undeferrable finitude of the old into jackets and blankets and hot infusions, into the adoration of their calloused hands and their eyes sunk in under their eyebrows, awareness of legacy, construction of a lineage that would fuse into universality. All of that the women brought: hyperbole and a hollowing out. That's what they brought if they let themselves look or be looked at, if they maintained his gaze – those pubescent women, those robust old women, those college kids a few seconds before plunging into the salt water, in those days, those first days of a vacation that had been, until then, perfect, and disappointing.

The women passed like Huns along the seashore. They'd pass by and leave the countryside devastated behind them. The women would pass, look, or hold his gaze an instant before plunging in. They'd pass, and the old Sherpa, still young, would feel very little, would feel next to nothing; he would look at his ankles barely grazed by dark seaweed. The faint current that returns, the wet sand, and its roughness. The regurgitation of the ocean mass: the ebb. The women would pass, and the Sherpa would return.

Slowly. Dragging the soles of his feet to that indeterminate point of the peninsula where he had left his towel, books, sunglasses, case, money, flip-flops, t-shirt. He'd return, the sea behind him, head bowed, no longer seeing anyone, terrified of himself, but even more so of those women who were passing, letting themselves look and be looked at, who enjoyed looking and feeling looked at; frozen stiff and soaking wet, in dormant and absolute terror, a terror of no consequence to the world; he'd return in an abyss of that autonomous terror, in the solipsism of that black hole-facing terror. He'd walk back, covering a few metres, not many, those it took to walk from the waves' edge to his towel, eyes on the sand, without raising his gaze; he no longer cared about looking at anyone, nor about the discomfort of his wet bathing suit and its frictions; he didn't care any more if the pages of his book were destroyed by the droplets that fell from his hair. All there was was his return, from the sea to that illusory island demarcated by five or six possessions. A t-shirt turned insufficient pillow, sunglasses, a book, money, flip-flops. The abstraction of a territory delimited for itself between the dunes and the horizon. He'd return to legislate that scant homeland founded upon sand, where he could stretch out on his towel: banner or flag, or capital city perhaps, of that sterile country where the old Sherpa, who was so far neither Sherpa nor old, could always return, more and more fed up with self-pity, that vice.

Face in the sand on the beach. The heat that dissipates. First in the air. Then in his own body. Finally, in the sand: in its crystals, in the pulverised minerals. The extinction of the sunlight, gradual; another circadian cycle to the measure of senility. Old Japanese people sliding rice paper doors. Until it is night, or until – at least – night can be called night. And there is no longer any point in hiding his head in the sand. The cosmic order informs the old Sherpa that it's time to go, to leave the beach, to seek another habitat. It tells him that the day has exhausted its splendour, and that it is time to take refuge: sheets, air conditioning, pale blue tablets to fight the mosquitoes. The book, if his diurnal frustration hasn't overwhelmed him completely, can accompany him. Reading forty to sixty pages and going back to sleep. But first he will have to stop by the corner store. Stock up on the essentials to make it to the next morning's breakfast at the hotel. Buy a soft cheese. Three slices of some cold cuts on promotion. Less, less than that. Only what's strictly essential. Mineral water? Less, less: there is a glass in the hotel bathroom and a magnanimous tap from which turbid water flows, but how turbid can water be, and how damaging can turbidity be from such a magnanimous tap next to the glass in the bathroom at the hotel?

So the old Sherpa goes: he walks though the ebbing streets of the peninsula towards a corner store. In flip-flops. Before – long before – the mountain summoned him by virtue of its volume, its massiveness. Before that orographic flight, those Himalayan slopes, the old Sherpa walks to the corner store: a yogurt with granola. Less, less: a fleshy fruit, just a sliver of a seasonal fruit. What's essentially strict. He shouldn't even go, the old Sherpa feels. If in eleven hours he can wake up and have breakfast. He doesn't need anything. But he is already on his way, and it is difficult for him to stop that inertial movement: make a decision, a different decision, an opposing one. It is preferable, then, to go by the corner store and purchase the minimum, the superfluous. Less: a spool of white thread for sewing. Less, less: a cotton swab, if they were to sell them individually.

The old Sherpa gets to the corner store: he goes straight to the fridge with the dairy products. He does not say hello, doesn't let himself be distracted. He chooses a chocolate dessert. He looks up. No one's there. Nor are there security cameras. In the solitude of the aisle, he resolves to be provocative. He takes the products off the shelves and examines them as though genuinely thinking of taking advantage of this lack of oversight to hide and steal them. But there is nobody watching him, nor anybody letting him watch them, or enjoy watching, and so he puts everything back on its shelf. Because there's no one.

Except her. There, next to the cash register, sitting on a tall, rickety stool. The old Sherpa will later learn: her name is Rabbit. She is crying.

Sixty-Six

'Shall we get up?' the old Sherpa hears at the exact moment when, contemplating the figure of the fallen Englishman, he was already thinking that he would never find a way to reconcile his desire for egalitarianism with his misanthropy. So he responds:

'Sure.'

Heathrow

The third of July, 1953, Heathrow Airport. It's summer in London. Photographers immortalise the arrival of the Himalayan heroes. The New Zealander Hillary wears a tie and a light, fashionable, fitted suit with three buttons, but only one is done up. The Sherpa Norgay, a shirt with the sleeves rolled up, the collar open, carrying a British flag in his right hand. He raises it and smiles. It is hard to find a photo of Norgay in which he isn't smiling. Always willing, always loyal. In the last stage of the ascent, he saved Hillary's life. And now the two of them are moving down the runway at the London airport. Dignitaries and personalities greet them, congratulate them. Right then the New Zealander is named Knight Commander of the Order of the British Empire, the first of the seven distinctions that the United Kingdom will grant him in the coming years. Norgay is given a medal with the likeness of King George VI, the stutterer.

Sixty-Eight

From the age of ten to the age of fourteen, the young Sherpa listened to National League broadcasts on the radio every Sunday. Of the nine teams that make up the Nepalese football association, he has a soft spot for the Three Star Club, The Patanites of Lalitpur, and for their cobalt jerseys. After, on spring and summer evenings, he would go out to play ball under the influence of that day's results. Sometimes with a couple of friends, but also alone, or with the walls of the houses. Even, from time to time, with some of the Europeans who for some incomprehensible reason believe that playing football with a Nepalese boy in the middle of the Himalayas is a sublime experience. That's when the tourists understand that, due to the domination of the incline, negotiations with the spherical aren't so easy when you live in the high mountains. But the young Sherpa was always a persevering boy. He still is.

What about studying something with more of a connection to our habitat? he wonders now. Urban planning, protecting the environment? He has always been very sensitive to his surroundings, his teachers never seem to tire of praising his curiosity, his ties to the external world. In fact, at this very moment his focus shifts from vocational uncertainty to the immediate: the Englishman and his sojourn on that ledge, fatal or providential, on the southern slope of the giantess.

Sixty-Nine

"**D**oes Shakespeare leave anything to chance? Flavius questions the first of the citizens: 'what trade art thou?' 'Carpenter,' the man answers. And that's when Marullus reprimands him for not sporting his leather apron and rule, the insignias of his profession. Then the cobbler comes in with his annoying puns. But I don't want to get too far ahead. I'd like for us to pause on that first citizen, who only says one thing throughout this whole work: 'Why, sir, a carpenter.' Of course, the author could have opted for any other profession: there were hundreds in both Ancient Rome and Elizabethan England. He could have said innkeeper, slave trader, freedman, tailor. But Shakespeare chooses carpentry. Was this by chance?

"There is only one famous carpenter dynasty in the history of literature: Joseph and his wife Mary's son. Is it by chance that Joseph and Mary were themselves persecuted by the very same empire that Flavius and Marullus are representing in the first scene of Julius Caesar? Perhaps. Or perhaps the playwright is making a point: it isn't the first time that the agents of Rome, holders of military and political power, officials of the Temple, administrators of exegetical knowledge, despise those carrying a transcendent message. It should be recalled that when Jesus was still a teenager, he already preached in the form of parables in front of the synagogue, and those who understood the Law were surprised by his insights, so much so they disregarded him completely. 'Isn't this the carpenter's son? Where then did this man get all these things?' the rabbis asked in the Gospel of Matthew.

"Just one line is uttered by this first citizen: 'Why, sir, a carpenter.' And *carpenter* is the Word of the Lord. Does Flavius know this? Yes, as a character in a tragedy written in the sixteenth century. No, as a Roman tribune far removed from the Judean upheaval of the first century. That ambiguity, that knowing and not-knowing of Flavius, young actor, must be summed up in a gesture. What gesture? Don't ask me: that is your art."

Seventy

The young Sherpa has yet to fully define how to feel before the immobilised body of the Englishman. On the one hand, he does not feel even an iota of guilt. There is no way he can be blamed for this novice's collapse. And yet, at some point deep down in his consciousness, almost inaccessible, he also perceives that manifesting an absolute indifference is also incorrect. Yet he feels no sadness, no dismay. He doesn't even really know this tourist who lies there with his head pointing west. There is no emotional bond, there is no anxiety. His professionalism is beyond a shadow of a doubt. Astonishment would be improper here: it's Everest; people fall all the time. So what? He doesn't know. He can't quite think.

If he were to ask the old Sherpa about all of this, the answer would be that in the face of other people's misfortunes, the typical response is compassion. A dormant sentiment that contributes nothing other than a certain lukewarm identification with the person suffering. The zero degree of the gregarious spirit. Recognise one's own limitations in the catastrophe of one's neighbour and sympathise with the species. Another key word: commiseration. Another: pity. But none of these possibilities is considered by the young Sherpa. It is not that he puts them to one side: they don't even occur to him. He has too pragmatic a temperament. And he's young. He sits down again (he was previously standing), and again he indicates the precipice. Without looking at him, he asks the old Sherpa:

'What if we go down?'

It's a stupid idea. The young Sherpa knows it, the old Sherpa knows it, everyone knows it. An unnecessary risk. It would have been different if, instead of three, the expedition had had four members, or twelve, or fifteen, as usual. In the face of whatever reiteration of misfortune, there would still be two (or ten, or thirteen) men standing. One to stay, another to seek help. In any case, the old Sherpa doesn't answer him right away. Not that he's considering the possibility of attempting a rescue descent. That is absolutely not an option. He just takes a moment to think of the best way to tell his partner that his idea makes no sense. That's why he delays several seconds, during which time the silence of the mountain recovers its protagonism. If the thunderous hum of hundreds of turbines from the underworld blowing icy air between the peaks of the Himalayas can be considered silence.

'No,' the old Sherpa finally responds. 'Because if I stay here…'

'True,' interrupts the young Sherpa. 'Better not.'

Strike

The Sherpa assembly, gathered at Mount Everest Base Camp, rejected on 21 April, 2014, the compensation of three hundred and fifty dollars offered by the Nepalese government. 'We have decided to suspend all climbs for the remainder of the year to honour our fallen brothers,' the Sherpa spokesman announced. Simultaneously, the Ministry of Culture, Tourism, and Civil Aviation promised that 'mountaineering activities would resume safely in a couple of days.' The response from Everest: 'Under no circumstances. In all of history, this is the first Sherpa strike.'

That same day, Sherpa delegates conveyed to the government a list of thirteen demands. Among other points, they demanded an increase in their fees, a review of the life insurance system, and a social containment fund for emergencies financed with a percentage of the royalty that Nepal charges mountaineers for each ascent. They also demanded that a monument be erected in Kathmandu in honour of the sixteen dead. The Ministry received the request. It only agreed to the final demand: it promised to build a mausoleum. The strike, of course, went ahead.

The Dark of Day

Rabbit is something new in this landscape. Not the corner store. The peninsular corner store is known territory. Four, five days, perfect, disappointing, have proved sufficient for him to annex the shelves of suntan lotion, the fruit crates – their squad of flies with green or iridescent eyes – the prophylactics display, the seals of the mineral water bottles united in shoals of half a dozen atop the tiles... The corner store has already been circumscribed, its seventy-five square metres that the old Sherpa had invariably explored after sunset, for six, five, four days, to provision himself with something light, a low-fat yogurt, or less, less than that: a summer fruit, half a bag of raisins, a travel tube of toothpaste. The pantry was an acquired terroir, an adoptive home, a stable reference in his vacation routine. It was always there, in the same place, loyal, predictable: open doors, fluorescent tube lighting, refreshing halo of doorless refrigerators. All this, in an artificial but not less concrete way, already belonged to the old Sherpa.

But not Rabbit.

Until that night, the cash register had been operated by a sullen, monosyllabic man with a grey moustache.

Four, five days, maybe less, had been enough for him to grow accustomed to this man, like someone who gets used to a new traffic light on his daily journey. A man who didn't cause any problems, didn't get his change wrong, didn't get carried away in casual conversations with natives or with tourists. A forgettable man. The old Sherpa appreciated that. When he met Rabbit, he realised that was what he liked about the absent man: his insipidity. It would never have occurred to the young old Sherpa to ask the cashier with the grey moustache and hollow eyes his name. Nor to dedicate three seconds to the calculation of his age, for example. Nor to figure out if he was the owner or an employee of that corner store of seventy-five square metres. That night he understood that that tacit agreement between the two of them kept them at a happy remove. Each comfortable with the ignorance of the other.

Rabbit, on the other hand, was crying. Loudly.

Rabbit's sobs as detour. Rabbit and her abjection. Although it could be argued that every voyage already contains, in latent form, the possibility of its deviations. That they're never random. That nor are they predestined. But they are larval, that much is true. They are crouched in their embryonic cocoons. They float, foetal, on the trail of amniotic becoming. Waiting for a catalyst. Rabbit's sobs, for instance.

Why is Rabbit crying? the old Sherpa wonders as he studies the cash register in the distance. From the shelf where the white bread is stacked, the old Sherpa watches Rabbit crying and wonders why. Why is she crying so much? Does it matter? Ought he not ask first if the reason for her crying is pertinent (or better still: conducive to anything)? Or is the important thing that she's crying, and that's that? What he does know is how she's crying: inconsolably. There is no dam, although there is some modesty. Her elbows resting on the counter where the register is, her shoulder blades, their spasms, her face half covered by the palms of her hands holding her head up by her forehead. Her eyes unfocused on the tin. When Rabbit sheds a tear or some mucus (and she sheds a significant amount), it is pierced by the laser beams of the barcode reader. A flannel cloth ought to cover that emission of consistent red beams. Like the ones used to clean the dashboard of a car. Or to polish a stylish piece of furniture. A Louis XV secretaire, a Chippendale dresser. But the flannel has been misfolded. Wrinkled, useless. Rolled up into a ball on the shell of the scanner. The old Sherpa sees that from the distance of the baked goods shelf and wonders: Why is she crying so much she can't even pick up the flannel and cover up the laser beams that shoot through her tears falling one after the other on the tin counter of the cash register? Why?

The old Sherpa, who is still young, who has never set foot on Nepalese soil, nor been infected by summit lust, who has never guided anyone on a climb, needs to make a decision.

One option is to return the chocolate dessert to the refrigerator with the dairy products and walk out of the corner store in silence. Not disturbing her. Flee Rabbit's crying. Look for some other store, maybe a kiosk, or that supermarket that's farther away, that has more things, and there he could purchase his dinner, which is not a dinner in the full sense of the word, but more of a snack, something that will allow him to sleep through the night, until morning comes with its proclamation that now he

171

may copiously breakfast. That: tomorrow is another day. He'll be able to come back tomorrow, at that point, yes, he can come back, to this corner store, his corner store, which he has made his in five, four days of vacation, and he can indeed buy – tomorrow – his dinner in the dairy section of the refrigerator. A low-fat yogurt. Or less: a glass of milk.

The other option is to wait. Stand still next to the packages of white bread and wait. At some point, it occurs to the old Sherpa, Rabbit's crying will stop. Why not? He's in no hurry. And there's something beautiful about that kind of crying. Or about her. Or about both things, if she – Rabbit, the woman – can be called a thing, or just reified for a moment in order to place her in a list with her crying. So he will wait. Watch her and stand there until she's finished, until she's got it all out, emptied herself of her anguish, her desolation. Only then, when Rabbit has composed herself again and dried her tears on a disposable tissue, when she has blown her nose and recuperated the rhythm of her breath, only then, yes, will he walk the eight or ten metres that separate him from the cash register and hand her his chocolate dessert. And pay. Perhaps an empathetic look. And leave.

It could also be a possibility, a third possibility, to walk to the cash register slowly, with caution. A lioness approaching the wildebeest lapping at the shore of the nocturnal pond. Gently rest the dessert on the tin. Wait whatever it takes for Rabbit to stop crying. Or at least until her eyes are no longer sunk in the palms of her hands and she raises her reddened eyes. And then, yes, he could ask, 'Are you okay?'

But the old Sherpa doesn't wait for Rabbit to stop crying. Nor does he look at her empathetically, nor does he silently flee and leave the corner store behind him. Of course, the old Sherpa does not sneak up stealthily to the cash register, nor does he face Rabbit, her irritated eyes, their spillage. Least of all does the Sherpa ask if she's okay, if she needs anything, if he can help her... Instead, he decides to act natural. The worst artifice. The old Sherpa, in the prime of his youth, resolves to act as though nothing were happening. A mise en scène of normalcy. The old Sherpa justifies his actions, of course. Somehow he senses the havoc to come and tries to find arguments. *It isn't that I'm indifferent to this pain. It isn't that her sadness doesn't move me... Quite the contrary: I am looking for the right way to scrupulously respect the intimacy of her catharsis,* he tells himself.

He walks the eight, ten, eleven metres to the cash register and hands her the chocolate dessert as if nothing out of the ordinary were happening. As if crying, even this way, the way Rabbit is crying, with irreparable grief, crying like the Sherpa has never seen in anyone before, were an everyday possibility in the tombola of human reactions. As if there were nothing to remark, nothing to emphasise. He hands over his chocolate dessert, observes its transit before the barcode reader and looks for the money in his sunglasses case. He doesn't rush. He pays, without it implying an avoidance of Rabbit. No, no. Quite the contrary: the old Sherpa looks at her. He sees her with her runny nose that she wipes with the sleeve of her blue apron. He sees her attempt to compose herself, the sob, the damp tissue, wrinkled between her fingers. As though nothing had happened. He gets his dessert back then. Refuses the green plastic bag. Says:

'Bye.'

He leaves. He takes two, four, five steps. He stops and runs back:

'You wouldn't happen to have a spoon, would you?'

The spoon is a bit big. At least in relation to the packaging of his dessert. Why might she have been crying? And why in that way? Who can cry like that? Was not her kind of crying a bit excessive, too? It's chilly. She'll feel better soon, thinks the old Sherpa. Whatever it is, she's probably feeling better about it by now. He tells himself he was right: why should he have bothered her? All these bugs that flit around the street lamps – what do they do during the day? Are they moths? Are they all moths? The same moths that eat clothes? The old Sherpa thinks how he doesn't know anything. Seriously, he asks himself: what could he have done? The sun was strong on the beach. The sea must be lukewarm now, this evening. Regulator of temperatures. Like crying. Isn't crying also a regulator of temperatures? Doesn't it help everything recover its equilibrium? What if he changes course and goes back to the beach and gets in the water now, when no one else will be there? But crying like that: she was pretty, that cashier. Even crying. Or was she pretty because she was crying? But afterwards it will be cold, and there will be no one to hand him a towel, he thinks. Besides, it's windy. On the sea it's always windy. He'd be better off heading back to the hotel. Dessert and a little reading, and then he'll fall asleep. Should he have said something to her? he wonders. What if she took it badly. He'll take a shower. A few spoonfuls of dessert first, and then get in the shower. Perhaps save a few spoonfuls for when he gets out of the shower. These people are Italians: he saw them on the beach today, he thinks, and indicates them with his eyebrows. They were speaking Italian, he heard them saying *tredici* at some point. It's also not like she said anything to him. He's not even from here. They don't know each other. He reaffirms: he did the right thing. They'd need to be small spoonfuls, half spoonfuls at a time, so that it lasts. It's cold. The Italians must be used to it. If they're Piedmontese, for example… Or do the Piedmontese speak in dialect? Are numbers different in dialect? He doesn't know anything, he thinks. Or maybe he's sick? He shouldn't be walking around in flip-flops. Were her eyes light? Is it true that eyes get lighter when you cry? And is it true that birds' eyes don't have retinas? Or do they not have corneas, lenses, pupils? He could have asked her something, of course; but what? What would his angle have been? Would it make sense to go back? He's hungry. The little dessert is very little. No matter how long he makes it last, the issue is not the volume of the spoonfuls but rather the quantity of dessert. But what does that mean? He goes back and buys more and says something to her? It's because it's cold that he's hungry. Just half a block left. Why would he go back? Had he been right? If he'd been her, would saying nothing have been right? Of course, what would he have said? He was definitely right. Or is it that birds are completely blind? What can you say, if he were her, what would people have said to him? The water must be warmish. If somebody would hold his towel out when he re-emerged. In this cold.

'Room one thirty-three, please,' the old Sherpa picks up his key at the desk.

Why Everest? Why not a local mountain range, why not the pantanal? The old Sherpa led his wandering mind to the lap of the mother of the world with the sea still in his sights. But not the gigantism of transoceanic currents. Not the generality of the planisphere, the blue splotch between two ochre outlines. He was escaping, more specifically, high tide. From the method of high tide. That way of occupying territory by means of vacillations. A wave that falls on the exact limit of the coast and pushes it half a metre farther. Does it take it by force? Does the high tide then establish – oh, *animus iocandi* – the beachhead? No. No way. The high tide advances and, no sooner has it achieved its expansion, it immediately retreats into the depths. Shy, almost sorry for having exceeded the conquest of terra firma. As if it feared the irate retaliation of dry land, as if the mineral kingdom had once punished it with the atavistic ferocity of the leader of the horde. Like a child, boy or girl, who for the first time pets the neck of a Percheron and withdraws the instant they've touched the mane for fear of the animal's reaction. Yet the retreat is brief. A fleeting demi-plié, a bow that seems humble and immediately reveals itself as cunning. Because a new wave is already mounting, organic and geometric, irrepressible and programmatic, in the same retractable gesture. The second wave crashes, and its foam: another half metre. The beach narrows a little more. The empire of salt expands through its liquids. Again: withdrawal, hypocrisy, violence, occupation. High tide, the conquest of a Creation predicated upon backward steps.

The ocean advances, then, over the habitable world, while the old Sherpa consumes his chocolate dessert on the bed in room one thirty-three at the peninsular hotel. He did not go back to the corner store where Rabbit was crying. This mortifies him. His selfishness. He was not right. He feels dejected by his inanity, his insignificance. All bad. He is ashamed of his stolidity, his cowardice. Would it have been that hard to talk to her? Of his lack of interest, his individualism. Why Everest? How hard would it have been to ask her if she needed something? Why not the salt flats or jungle? The ocean advances upon the solid, inundates it, makes it soft and pale, dissolves its pigments. The old Sherpa feels his strength leaving him. He lies back. How hard would it have been?

Now the old Sherpa is sleeping. And once he gets started it's hard to get him to stop. It's addictive. It's a different type of sleep. Sleep as training for a morphean decathlon. Sleeping a lot. Sleeping more and more each day. Ten, twelve hours. Half the day away, in the beginning. But then that's no longer sufficient. It's tiring to sleep once you've surpassed the level of the neophyte. It is physically exhausting. Destructive to the psyche. Sleeping fourteen, fifteen hours, every day. It's like exiting the planetary orbit, the astral reference. Down, before, after… The simplest ideas start to lose their meaning. Spatial ideas, for example. Sleeping seventeen hours and waking up: today, tomorrow, still… It's dark. Time becomes inelastic: it cracks at the slightest movement, becomes fragile. His legs have got weak, as well. His eyelids puffy. The old Sherpa lies back down. Closes his eyes. Just for a little while. He gets up. Hair plastered against his skull. It's dark now, too. Before? How can it already be dark out? Sleeping twenty hours, for example. Go down to have breakfast, but he can't, because 'it's five-thirty', the concierge tells him. Not any more, or not yet? Five-thirty of which night? So the old Sherpa goes back to his room. Tired. *Tredici*? Exhausted. He's thirsty. His back, calves, neck, head hurt. He sits on the bed. He gets up and opens the blinds: it's dark. He closes them. He sits back down on the bed. He wakes up. He had fallen asleep. He goes down to have breakfast. No: not now. 'There's no service,' says the concierge. But how can that be? Did he say service? Is it still dark outside? Doesn't seem like it. He would say it's the middle of the morning. A normal day. Or almost. Why was it that girl was crying, sitting on her stool, its back given out? Was it something that could have been avoided? It's not the usual light. Perhaps a solar eclipse, with its rarefied effulgence, the faint interlining of the veil that's ineffective at hiding the glare. Is it an eclipse then? Or not any more? The corpuscles floating around the old Sherpa are darkening again. 'What about now?' he asks. 'Is there service now?' But the concierge doesn't understand. There's no one else. Where is everyone? On the beach? Did they decide to go to the beach tonight? The frosted glass door that thickly separates the hotel from the street shows a pale light at one corner. An obvious but elusive source of glare. Is it the sun? Five-thirty? Whose? Is everyone at the beach on this radiant morning? The splotch of light blurs its contour in the dirty pattern on the green glass. One of the municipality's lanterns? Is it the sun behind a dense layer of cirrus clouds that announce rain on the peninsula? Is it the reflection of an internal light, a floodlight from the lobby oriented wrong? The radiant flux sinks a little more. From what sunset come those opacities that arise between the concierge desk and the desire to have breakfast that hits hard, falling like asbestos curtains? Who emits the dark of day?

The old Sherpa is thirsty. His head, calves, back ache. 'Would you like a wakeup call once breakfast starts?' asks the concierge who is half helpful and half despicable. His eyelids are covered in a slimy patina, lacrimal secretions, the weight of the days. Was that girl at the corner store crying, or was it the Sherpa who was crying? The concierge looks at him: he's judging him. The Sherpa is annoyed by the grammar in the concierge's phrasing: '…once breakfast starts'. As if the breakfast were voluntarily offering itself to the heterophagy of tourist contingents. But he doesn't say anything. That's not true: 'Sure, please,' says the old Sherpa, who isn't a Sherpa yet. Or old. He wants to be woken up for breakfast, for the first breakfast there is. 'Room?' asks the concierge. It's exhausting to sleep twenty, twenty-two hours a day, every day, all his dreams blank. Waking loses sharpness.

Nothing is diaphanous any more: not sleep, not waking. Everything takes on laxness and imprecision. Is the room already paid for? Where is his credit card with its sixteen digits, its magnetic stripe? No, no. No, no. That isn't what you're being asked. The old Sherpa's eyes close. He loses sight of the concierge for a moment, and a number. One thirty-three. 'One thirty-three,' he answers. The concierge notes it down phlegmatically. And the Sherpa turns and stumbles to the elevator door. He presses the button even though it's already on the ground floor. He waits a few seconds. Annoyed, he clicks his tongue. He drags himself to the staircase. He climbs eighteen steps, puts the key in his lock. He staggers two, three steps. He collapses on the bed. Now the old Sherpa is sleeping. And, in his dream, Rabbit is crying.

Seventy-Three

The Englishman still lies rigid on the mountainface, and the old Sherpa can imagine him already connected to a multitude of prosthetic devices. Nothing complicated: a cast, an intravenous pain reliever, the drip of the IV…

The IV, the old Sherpa thinks, is used less frequently than one might think. It's a fiendishly practical invention. It's impossible to comprehend how Fordism squandered its applications. It would have been ideal to place on industrial assembly lines. An IV drip for every worker. Communion around the provision of proteins that reaches the bloodstream of the working class and constructs a new society. Strong, hopeful. The women – their hair gathered up with clasps, with elastic bands, inside brightly coloured handkerchiefs – arrive at the factory, punch their cards, put their gloves on, place the catheter in their right forearm, and a new day in the productive cycle has begun. Outside, the men, their wars, the Angelus Novus regarding the ruins of history… Ah, progress. What little has been done on its behalf.

Seventy-Four

The very day they arrive in London, at Heathrow international airport itself, a press conference. A journalist asks about the moment of the expedition when Norgay saves Hillary's life. The New Zealander expresses once more his gratitude towards the Sherpa. He speaks of his reflexes and mettle. Norgay scratches his chin, thoughtful, circumspect. Journalists listen in reverent silence to the account of that critical moment. Then they ask Norgay how he felt when he reached the top of the world. He answers at least eight words in Nepali. An interpreter translates laconically: 'He was very happy.' And all of them – Hillary, the journalists, the translator, Norgay himself – burst out laughing. As though that happiness, or even the mention or the chance of that happiness, could only result in uncontrollable laughter.

But one of the journalists takes offense. Guilty, vindictive, he approaches Norgay. He asks him: 'Don't you feel, Mr. Tenzing, that you are being discriminated against? Don't you think that you, too, a Sherpa, ought to have been made a Knight of the Realm by Her Majesty? Did you not reach the same summit as Edmund Hillary? Do you not think, Mr. Tenzing, that the Crown of Great Britain and the whole of the West have done an immense injustice to you for purely racial reasons?' Norgay responds: 'Would a knighthood give me wings?'

Seventy-Five

The old Sherpa's mind was wandering. Not remembering, not thinking, not silently performing a melody, not looking for the right word. It could be said that it was floating – through bits and pieces of images, scraps of disconnected phrases. Then the young Sherpa asked him:

'What if we go down?'

Starting with that question the old man resigned himself, with anticipated nostalgia, to abandoning that state of drifting consciousness and launched the shortest possible process of evaluation, in order to find the best way of saying:

'No. Because if I stay here…'

But now that this dialogue wound up prematurely in the past, the old Sherpa would like to go back to that sort of waking slumber, to the free reflections of that placid daydream that had taken him far from the mountain and the fallen tourist. Nevertheless, this seems impossible. He remembers nothing. It has all been buried in the most opaque of oblivions. Buried at a depth where acids or alkalis conspire against any and every form of life. Not the fertile earth, teeming with subterranean life, but the barren, sulphurous, hot, dead mineral plates. The images that had for a moment succeeded in distracting the old Sherpa from his painful circumstances, from his new failure to attain the top of the mountain have sunk that far. He makes one more effort to find a clue, the strand of a thread that might lead him to the Minotaur's house, all corridors and a central room, a considerable draught.

'True,' answers the young Sherpa's voice. 'Better not.' And that sound is also a shove to the older man's consciousness that allows him to reencounter an image: a bus stop, one autumn day, the first afternoon that he came home alone from school. A confused feeling, a mix of pride and abandonment. But that recollection didn't last at all, it had immediately merged into the memory of a girlfriend, or not even a girlfriend, but the semi-darkness of a room where a young woman is sleeping, a woman who is going to say no to being his girlfriend, and the strangeness of walking naked through someone else's house. But there was more: another woman, a different woman, crying. A woman crying behind a cash register, and also a man sitting in an armchair…

But not everything can be recovered. Things don't respond very gracefully to will. The old Sherpa cannot reconstruct the chain of images and sounds that had turned him into a sleeping funambulist, in the same way that the young Sherpa cannot recover, by simple volitional impulse, the humanity of the Englishman who rests on a ledge, on a marginal bluff, on a Nepalese mountain.

Seventy-Six

Which means, the young Sherpa realises, there's nothing for it but to wait. But he doesn't imagine an ecstatic vigil, nor anxiety for an imminent resolution. They are not two little boys under a Christmas tree ten minutes before midnight. If he wanted to look for an analogy, he would really have to think of someone next to a coffee vending machine. You put in the coins, you press the button, and you let time pass. Not much. Thirty, forty seconds, until the mechanism stops. Only then does the little door open so you can take the plastic cup. Those stirring sticks aren't spoons. They've thought of everything, down to even that detail, to make sure we accept that what we are consuming is not really coffee, but rather some substitute, an homage.

Wait a while longer: after all, not so much time has passed. Twelve minutes? Fifteen? Not an excessive amount. This could still be considered a minor accident, an episode that – adorned appropriately – focuses the attention of family members having dinner together. The young Sherpa manages to dedramatise the matter for a moment. It's a stumble, a bang on the head, a passing dizzy spell, and then they'll get back on track. Are we going to reach the summit in these conditions? But of course: this is no big deal at all. At all. A slip. In a little while we'll be skipping along the slope with the oxygen cylinders on our backs. Flying. We will be agile, determined. It will be heart-warming to see our light feet overcome with ease the limitations of our movement. We will laugh. We will skip, laugh, and climb. Without stopping, without stumbling. One foot and then another, closer with every passing second to the end. Night will fall, and we will sleep a deep sleep, soft and undisturbed. The sleep of the serene in the stuffed animal factory, the night they have brought their opium pipe, too. The next day we will contemplate the planet from its top.

Of course it is only a second, a gust of anaesthesia that relieves the sorrow of seeing the Englishman down below, lying on the rock, lost in his gravid corporeity. It's a brief moment before the word is returned to the box of the irreversible, before it makes itself present with its flotilla of tragic predestinations. A regrettable loss, a true disaster. The life of a man. A young man, with enormous potential, intrepid, full of projects. A life in full bloom suddenly cut down by the bloodlust of the giantess, of this mineral titan indifferent to the fragility of mortals. Another existence reduced to the germinal point of senselessness, another proof of the pompous futility of human destiny. The young Sherpa feels terrible. He takes his eyes off the abyss.

Digestion

A few metres from the Englishman's motionless body, the older man is still processing the piece of chicken he tore into with his teeth the night before, misplacing some of the bird's skin between incisors and premolars. *Digestion...*, the old Sherpa thinks. A primitive mechanism that wears down the teeth and shakes up the entrails. He'd like the tourists to witness his digestive processes up close. Show them to them, they who are so sensitive to naturalist allegories. They who get besotted by any story with a holm oak or a wild hare as minor characters. They who dream all the time of the tender pastures of March, the succulent stags of autumn served up on the grass for predators' fangs.

Tourists, the old man thinks, invented the superiority of the immaculate, of the virgin. They cannot understand the beauty of the wheat field polished by the hand of man; they do not enjoy the subject of history cast upon the environment, ploughing and reaping according to the logic of terrestrial translation. They evoke a pre-social dimension, confident in the weakness of organisation; they long for a time when inequities were resolved by blood in favour of the animal best endowed for the fight.

Learn this, the old Sherpa would say to them: that chicken died by human hands. There was premeditation; there was a plot. Malice aforethought. The tourists feel comfortable eliding those details. But they are part of the virtuous circle of extermination that brings poultry production to their plates, to their yellow and green tin bowls on the southern slope of the giantess, a few metres from where the Englishman suffers his immobility.

Seventy-Eight

After the Sherpa strike broke out, nearly four hundred tourists who had already paid for their expeditions were stranded at Base Camp. Mountaineers expressed their indignation on the net: 'The tribute to the dead Sherpas was distorted by the intervention of militant groups and turned into a political rally,' said one in an interview with a British newspaper.

An Australian filmmaker, Jennifer Peedom, was in the mountains shooting a documentary when the cessation of activities was declared. In a sequence from her film *Sherpa*, Peedom records a discussion between a Westerner and the owner of the travel agency she had hired. On seeing that the Sherpas didn't want to go back to work, desperate, the tourist pleaded with the intermediary: 'And... can't you talk to their owners?' The word he uses is *owners*. He says it in English. In German it probably would have been *Herrschaft*, as in *Herrschaft und Knechtschaft*, as Hegel liked to say. 'Can't you talk to their owners?'

The Old Sherpa

Why not the desert or the estuaries? Why not the fertile charm of the prairie? Why the mountain? It might be because on the mountain there are no phones. The old Sherpa feels the cold saliva beyond his mouth. The stupor. The phone rings in his room at the peninsular hotel. He opens an eye. The other is against the pillow. Only one eye open, then. But not for too long: he soon loses his vigour, the eyelid cedes, and the pupil clouds into the dome of the eye socket. Hibernation. The telephone rings. It's cold. Air-conditioning, thinks the old Sherpa. And the alert eye is activated anew. It seeks its objective on the horizon of the sheet and finds the glacial mouth of Boreas, open in a frigid nineteen-degree grimace. It felt colder. The phone rings, and the old Sherpa picks up the receiver. The result is agreeable. It isn't silence: it is rather the cessation of that sound. A hushed stridency in the middle of a hysterical crisis. A poultry bird that dies without feeling any pain, when a passenger plane falls on top of it. On the mountain there occasionally are, in fact, poultry birds. Chickens, some geese. Wild, of course. The bar-headed geese, for example, that migrate from India to Mongolia, ascending out of control above the mountain range, against all instinct for self-preservation. But the old Sherpa isn't on the mountain, but rather at sea level. Or one storey above sea level. In room one thirty-three, where the phone stops ringing in the same instant that he remembers Rabbit, with her inconsolable tears, the languid way she passed the chocolate dessert through the barcode reader, the red lasers tracing the tracks of her left hand, the plastic spoon she gave him at the wrong time and in the wrong size, his return to the hotel, his guilt, the everlasting night that never led to breakfast, and the hieratic concierge who announced that no, that not yet, still, not any more was there breakfast for the estimable guest because in some way that was mysterious, or perhaps completely incomprehensible, Rabbit's weeping had slipped the old Sherpa out of the usual flow of linear chronology, had taken him to another site where nothing was possible but to sleep, to indulge without pleasure in the suspension of consciousness, and to drag himself – univalve, gastropod – through the lowest level of existence. Until the phone rang, the old Sherpa answered, basked in the cessation of the ringing and, simultaneously, as if waking, answering, enjoying, and self-flagellating were all a single action, he recalled Rabbit's weeping, his own indifference, his indolent way of paying her, saying a single syllable to her as he went out… He remembered how, in the epitome of cynicism, he went back a few metres to demand (reproach her for the lack of) a plastic spoon.

'Good morning, señor, from the front desk.'

'Yes?'

'I'm so sorry to disturb you, but we have the breakfast ready now.'

'Who?'

'The breakfast buffet is open now, señor. You had asked us to let you know.'

The old Sherpa hangs up the phone, still lying face down. He recognises the day, assumes his geolocation: the peninsula, his vacation, the morning. And he believes for a little while – the time it takes him to put on his flip-flops, go down the stairs, stain the tablecloth, tire of the baked goods – that things have started over. That he'll go back to the beach, that the wheel has reacquired its circularity: sleep, breakfast, sleep, beach, read, sleep, sea, sleep… Eat. A little. What's necessary. Some tropical fruit. Or less. Less than that: a dried fig. Some cranberry juice. He believes that yes, he will go back to his seaside routine of disdaining the idleness of others until the women prevail. Until it's impossible to ignore them. Until they (light, plump, half-naked, carefree) pass by, look at him, enjoy looking and being looked at, and until they remind the old Sherpa of his pathological isolation, his libidinal incapacity, his affective idleness. He believes in this, in the reestablishment of a soothing routine, in the repetition of the scheduled shipwreck. This is the illusion: the spurious rearing of hope and fraud. A short-haul squab. The premature phoenix of the folk tale: a bird that just barely survives its birth only to immediately die. At every moment.

But the illusion evaporates with breakfast. It dissipates as soon as his blood glucose levels rise. Because all the shadow puppets of the morning theatre, those hunch-backed creatures, end up drowned in Rabbit's crying.

Rabbit still cries among the crumbs on the stained tablecloth, among the ruins of a ravenous breakfast. She laments his gluttony, nutritional obverse of greed. She collapses in sobs and convulsions next to the tropical fruit that's on offer to the tourist. Next to the orange juice. And the coffee. The buns, the croissants. The strawberry jam, the scrambled eggs. The bacon. Every time the old Sherpa remembers the moment when, absenting himself, he said, 'Bye.'

Rabbit's tear ducts flood, inundations, deluges, arks without crews that run aground on grey shorelines, arks without an ounce of biodiversity in their holds. Ghost arks that don't even transport cadavers, but are rather artefacts of technical abstraction, that float and drift in Rabbit's weeping until they crash empty against their Ararat, every time the old Sherpa recalls the final instant when he asked: 'You wouldn't happen to have a spoon, would you?'

Sheer deluge among the remains of a breakfast in a peninsular hotel. Sleep, breakfast, sleep, beach, read, sleep, sea, sleep… Never again. Stripped of the dazzle of its shell, the illusion exaggerates his eyes; his lungs well up with water. Now what? Now the illusion floats there, dead, and the old Sherpa bids farewell to his Ophelia, downriver. That river, now the mouth, now frank maritime expansion, filters its humidity from the buffet into the lobby, the carpeted staircase, up to the door of room one thirty-three, up to the bed and the sheets still rumpled lying in wait for the daily service. The old Sherpa collapses in bed. His head to one side, eyes open, staring at the beige curtains of the hotel. Minutes pass; the old Sherpa doesn't want to sleep. He doesn't want to eat, doesn't want to go to the beach. He's lying down and breathing. His hands pressed together between his bent knees. His shoulders a little raised: later his neck will hurt, his calves, his head. He doesn't know whether to be cold or what. Whether to get under the covers, turn over. Whether to shut his eyes. For Rabbit to stop crying, is what the old Sherpa wants.

Now he's lying down. Without moving. Still. It could be said that stretching out the fingers of one hand or releasing for a second his jaw from the lock of bruxism is, in a certain way, changing position. But the proxemic approach is static: his right ear resting against the pillow, his knees pressing against the phalanges, legs doubled up, feet together on the dishevelled sheets of room one thirty-three.

He tries without much luck to stay awake. He dreams short dreams of low rhetorical density: practically lacking metonymy, metaphor exhausted. More like reviews of flat images, half coloured. Like someone who shakes the feather duster over the shelf, raising the dust so that it stays suspended in the air a few seconds and falls back onto ornaments: little tourist saucers from Swiss vacation houses, post-Columbian ocarinas, a family photo... Clinging to the bed, oblivious to the wide world and its sensuality, it is, for the old Sherpa, a way of flagellating himself. Falling asleep during his penitence is, in turn, a way of spoiling it.

His eyes burn. For the first time in hours, he moves one of his hands from between his knees, and the torture takes multiple forms: his hand hurts, his knee, his shoulder, the back of his neck. He rubs his closed eyelids with the same right hand. For a moment he stops looking at the beige curtains in the hotel room. In perplexion, his eyes rove over other points in space. He is aware that it is no longer morning. He is broken down and desperate.

Sitting on the bed, he sees a flip-flop on the floor peeking out from under the bedspread. He doesn't see the other one. He imagines it hidden by the mass of the mattress. But it's mere speculation. A hypothesis that will be disproved: the left flip-flop was next to the door. He feels like going to the bathroom. Yes, the bacon. Tropical fruit and coffee. The buns, the strawberry jam, the scrambled eggs. He gets up. He is standing. The mechanism works, he can make plans. He can go out.

Now on the street, the old Sherpa drags his flip–flops over the sandy gravel of the resort town. Tourists wander around anaesthetised by leisure, returning early from the beach, maybe planning on siestas. Looking for shade in the early afternoon, craving a late lunch, emanating fumes of sun protection. The old Sherpa lingers for a moment on that expression: sun protection. He thinks it could be a noble title in the proper empire. 'Sapa Inca, Viracocha's Chosen Brother and Great Sun Protector of the Tahuantisuyo.' The old Sherpa walks. Where are his footsteps taking him, those steps that are in fact the reptilian spasms of his flip–flops upon the barely perceptible tracks of the summer season? To the only site possible: the corner store, the little grocery, the summary supermarket. It isn't far. Even if it's still hot. It's the worst time of day. The most critical period for those summering: not morning, not dusk, not unbridled noctambulism. Afternoon: that moment when you have to make a determination. Leaving the beach enables the possibility of returning as sunset starts to scatter all its melancholy – at least as a plan. Staying forces you to carry on by the sea until the emergence of the first star. Take a siesta on the beach? That's what the old Sherpa could do if he weren't walking the few blocks that separate the hotel from the corner store; the Calvary on account of Rabbit's crying, which allows him to do nothing but sleep. He turns a corner and it's twenty metres, fifteen, seven. He hesitates. He under-stands the vulnerability of his idea: seeing Rabbit… Why? He does not deceive himself. He knows that this excursion is born of some new selfishness. Rabbit does not need to see him, Rabbit doesn't know him. As far as Rabbit's concerned, he's a chocolate dessert crossing the bar code reader on a bad night at the corner store. Seeing Rabbit is, to put it crudely, an exculpatory

operation. This atonement can only have one benefi-
ciary: the future Sherpa who now walks the streets of
the peninsula and enters the store.

Next to the cash register there is a man. Grey
moustache. He counts coins. He separates them, classifies
them, orders them.

The old Sherpa peeks in and sees the man with the grey
moustache who is absent-mindedly stacking up coins
on the tin of the counter next to the cash register. He
remains in that contemplative state for a moment. What is
he seeing? A usurper, a litigant who is occupying the site
of the desolation. There is an element of duel in the old
Sherpa's fantasy. A duel on the dusty street, abandoned
after the gold rush. There's no one else. Or is there? Is
that shadow that's moving past the spice shelf an old
woman in a black and gold bathing suit, or the inverted
reflection of the glow of the dunes? It doesn't matter:
it is something ethereal in any case, of a transience well
above average.

The old Sherpa pushes away his distractions and
focuses on the cashier. What does he see? He sees an
enemy, an opponent. Someone to defeat. He starts to walk,
in a straight line, from the door up to the register. This
manoeuvre, he believes, must necessarily disconcert his
adversary. Because cashiers, he reasons, have the atavistic
instinct to await frontal attack: the horde of consumers
who line up in front of their own trenches. They don't
even know the cashiers have a rear guard. They are like
pawns unaware of the reversible acrobatics of a knight,
the oblique vileness of the bishop, or the omnivorous
voracity of a queen.

Stealthily, the old Sherpa approaches. A metamor-
phosis: now he is in the Central African steppe. The

cheetah stalking the gazelle. Imperceptible footsteps on rubber flip-flops that avoid that drag, the irritating friction of the grains of sand that the carelessness of the tourists, unapprehensive, negligent, scatter around the peninsula. Two, three steps, and it all falls apart. An out-of-tempo exhalation, the excessive swinging of an arm, the impact of the shadow cast indoors, the grazing of the Bermuda shorts against the inner thighs... Or, to put it more plainly, the peripheral vision of the cashier with the grey moustache who notices an element that's out of place and pauses his count of those coins made out of nickel and raises his eyes.

There are two omissions that surprise the old Sherpa in that moment. That the cashier does not shoot him. That the cashier doesn't run out of the store. What follows, instead, is suspended sequentiality. A holding of the breath, a parenthesis. But it doesn't last. Immediately the world keeps going, and their eyes meet as they unite in the ambiguity of a mutual lack of recognition. The cashier looks at the Sherpa, who has yet to even dream of the Himalayas. His eyes are dull, yes, but they hide in their gelatinous beds a hint of intrigue. The Sherpa looks at the cashier and his pupils, in turn, reveal immediate terror.

The optic lasso forces the old Sherpa to take the next step. They can't keep looking at each other indefinitely. He feels like he's going to have to say something. Soon, now. To himself, with his mouth shut, he tries to start with a casual justification. An 'excuse me', a 'sorry', or, to take a more articulate route, a 'Just a quick question, if I may...' But he does not get to shape the conversation for two reasons. Firstly, he is paralysed by the impossibility of wrapping up his preamble. 'Excuse me,' what? Secondly, an older woman – dark bathing suit, detail of gold clasps on the front and back, high flip-flops, bluish makeup

– materialises in front of the cash register.

'Rabbit didn't come in today either?' she says to the cashier. 'What's going on with that girl? Is the baby all right?'

On the one hand, the old Sherpa gets the name: Rabbit. On the other, a bifurcation: who should he talk to now? With the cashier with the grey moustache or with the woman with the gold clasps on black Lycra? The official channel, the protocol, continues to lie with the man who occupies the sloping stool, almost without solder, where Rabbit spilled her tears with the incontinence of an overflowing reservoir. But the woman seems more accessible, more open, less reserved. Her name is Rabbit, then?

The old Sherpa resolves that he will talk with that older woman, a disagreeable idea to him, as well, of course, but in a different way. The cashier inspires an apprehension verging on violence. In a completely capricious way, the Sherpa believes that the cashier will wind up battering him in the face with one of the sets of inflatable arm bands on display at the entrance to the corner store. In his fantasy, in some homoerotic way, he – the Sherpa – must defend himself from the irascible employee of this store, and he ends up whacking him between the eyes with the base of one of the beach umbrellas stacked to the side of the fruit crates. Baby? Did someone mention a baby? The old Sherpa, in a gesture difficult for any passing witness to interpret, stops staring at the woman and the cashier, turns on his heels and walks out of the corner store.

Once he's outside of the supermarket, the old Sherpa simulates innocence and anticipates the apparition of the black Lycra and the gold clasps. He notes – without intending to – that on the sidewalk, in some display racks, the same store also offers books and postcards. The books don't attract him so much: a selection of bestsellers from the past twenty years in pocket, portable, inexpensive editions, with lots of commercial airliners on the covers, as well as some freedom fighters, here and there some silk fetish, too. Or nylon fetish. Or synthetic taffeta. The postcards, on the other hand, he finds disturbing. The postcards radiate disorder. A discovery would require a little process of intellection: is that not the Venetian Lido? And beside it, by contiguity, is that the St. Petersburg Hermitage? And the Pyramid of the Sun, in Teotihuacán? But even one step further: not only visual recognition, but also the finding of divergence.

That is, why on a beach in a subordinate country are postcards of tourist attractions so remote being sold? Does it count if you send your godmother a picture of Angkor Wat from the profanity of the postal service of this seaside resort? Is it not an injustice to the godmother who welcomed you in her arms while the priest poured cold and holy water on your bare head? The Sherpa takes four postcards at random and reviews their backs. The printing of all has the same origin: a printer dedicated to offset and headquartered in another coastal city that is larger, uglier, more industrious, richer. The legends and epigraphs are accurate: 'Megalithic Temple of Stonehenge, Wiltshire, England,' or 'Kruger National Park, Mpumalanga, South Africa.' The motifs multiply on the upper branches of the display. London, Rio de Janeiro, New York, the Iguazu Falls, and of course, the Himalayas.

The old Sherpa is fascinated by the postcards. He has a few in his hand, and, due to that fascination they inspire in him, he feels a little stupid. He tries to remember who'd said that humanity could be defined by – or that it found its key identifier in – its capacity to create secondary systems: tools that are used to make tools, codes with an aptitude for metalinguistic reflection, sexual regulations on progeny... But the old lady in the black and gold is already exiting the store:

'Just a quick question, if I may, madam...'

'You mean me?'

'Yes, please forgive me... Might you be able to tell me where miss Rabbit lives? It's just that I was supposed to bring her something, and today...'

'Today she didn't come to work.'

'Yes, exactly: I tried to come, but...'

'Is it something for the baby?'

'Yes, no... For the baby and for her.'

The woman looks at him. She sees the postcards in his hand. She accepts the improbable.

'Come with me,' she tells the old Sherpa. 'Take her the postcards; you can pay for them another time. No one ever buys them. And help me with my bag.'

How close to the sea does the bed or the kitchen of a house need be so that its inhabitants, without being misleading, can still say: 'Yes, I live on the coast'? At the very very edge of that estimate, the woman in black and gold and high-soled flip-flops, with her skinny calves and her commendable balance, delivers the old Sherpa to his fate. 'The house is there,' she tells him and points at nothing.

The west, or southwest, calculates the old Sherpa. There are trees, yes. Quite a number of them. Mostly eucalyptus. But also araucarias, cypresses. He thanks the old woman and returns her bag to her: a squash, powdered milk, chamomile tea, two cans of an energy drink, a colossal number of leeks. 'Leeks; onions are hard on my system, you get me? At my age,' she explains and hits her belly. He nods. He turns back to the trees. Eucalyptus all around. The occasional pink lapacho tree, too, a few ash trees, a pale cedar twisting its crown towards the sea that can neither be seen nor heard here. He thanks her again. He says goodbye. He sees no houses. Not in that direction. The old woman turns right and walks off with her bag from the corner store, leek stalks sticking out in the sun. There are no constructions on her horizon, either. This fills the Sherpa with hope. And so he walks. It is not time for climbs, for steep cliffs, not yet. That's some time away. Everything on the peninsula is plains. And the old Sherpa, who is still very young, walks. Seven, ten, thirteen minutes. The wind pushes him from behind; the design of the flip-flops begins to pierce his skin, to form a blister between his toes. It's still early. It is, it could still be said, afternoon. Or its death rattle. Summer evenings never quite finish starting, and the old Sherpa walks. Fifteen, nineteen minutes. Finally he sees it: a shack. Almost like a raised granary. But at ground level. A hut. Picturesque, austere, in its own way enchanting. Delimited by a colourless wooden fence. Varnished years ago. Two coats of marine lacquer that have already been eaten away by the salt air. The Sherpa gets closer: this has to be Rabbit's house.

As he advances, two perceptual epiphenomena. First, an old bicycle parked next to the door. Then, a dog that's almost blind that appears from somewhere with its hypertrophied sense of smell and howls in the direction of the old Sherpa. Then, yes, the mother lode: the door opens, and Rabbit comes out of the house. She's holding a baby in her arms. She isn't crying. The baby isn't, either.

Eighty

Is the situation of the Englishman anomalous? If a man tries to climb, against all common sense and every biological imperative, a mountain of 8,848 metres, what would be the norm? That he would survive, or that he'd die? You'd have to ask the Englishman, who has his maps with him, now lying alongside his immobile body, on a rock, his head pointing west, his legs at an ayurvedic angle.

Eighty-One

'Did he move?'

The old Sherpa has just said something and is pointing downward while looking childishly at his young colleague. He thinks he might have detected something: a tremor, a slight tremor in the right leg of the fallen man. And he is like a little boy who thinks he might have seen, through the window, the hump of a camel on Epiphany. He is elated, wants to share what he knows, to corroborate it, but at the same time to preserve the exclusivity of his discovery. The young Sherpa wasn't looking. He is incapable of answering.

'Huh?'

'I think he moved.'

The young Sherpa then peeks out again and sees the same eternal scene. A child of Great Britain stretched out on a rocky ledge, head pointing west, legs sketching the outline of a gabled roof ravaged by a storm. This vision, somehow, attenuates his previous judgments. Facing the materiality of the fallen body once more restores the situation to a more prosaic plane. The possibilities are binary again, without digressions. Alive or dead. Whatever it is, that body doesn't move.

'I don't think so.'

He says it gently, cautiously, without any intention of causing pain. The old Sherpa absorbs the impact. He thought he saw a leg timidly breaking the stillness of the Englishman. But, all in all, what difference would that make? Everyone knows about cadaverous spasms and the final sprint of the chickens fêting their acephaly. It doesn't add anything. It isn't information, it's white noise on the eardrum of the German radio operator in the middle of the bombing of Dresden.

'I just thought that maybe.'

The old Sherpa says that and gets up as though he's made a definitive decision. As though he were thinking of going straight back to his house now. With the attitude of someone who has resolved all matters in question and wants to move on. He gets up, takes a step back, dusts off his snow suit, stretches his legs. He gives the sense that he'll initiate the descent this very instant. But first he looks at the young Sherpa, who – concessive – tells him:

'Might have been the sun, a reflection. What about when it gets dark?'

Then, for a moment, silence dominates the path to the summit of Everest. If the furious race of monsoon winds blasting the outlines of the Nepalese mountain range can be considered silence.

Eighty-Two

"Flavius, then, walks through the streets of Rome with another tribune. They meet a mob of citizens who support Julius Caesar. They interrogate them, reprimand them, belittle them, accuse them of all kinds of things, and, in the end, attempt to win them over to their cause. What do the citizens do? They leave. Do they side with the murdered Pompey? Nobody knows. They just leave. Perhaps they simply tell the tribunes what they want to hear, then turn the corner and go back to rejoicing in the arrival of Julius Caesar. Maybe they just wanted to celebrate something. We don't know. Shakespeare himself doesn't seem to know.

"We do know what Flavius does once the mob has left. 'See whe'er their basest mettle be not moved,' he tells Marullus, indicating the citizens as they walk away. Is Flavius feeling self-satisfied here? Does he really believe that his speech was enough to move those plebeians? Perhaps it's all he has left, perhaps he can't conceive of any other possibility. Or maybe he's just strutting in front of Marullus, showing him that his eloquence is capable of changing the course of history. But it's a course, young actor, that is in fact rerouted by murder:

that of Pompey before the play begins, and that of Julius, at the start of the third act. Would it be appropriate to recall that famous sentence that posits violence as the midwife of history? We'd need to think about it; it's not a simple matter, nor an agreeable one. Let's go back to Flavius: 'See whe'er their basest mettle be not moved. They vanish tongue-tied to their guiltiness.' That's his line. The last he dedicates to the people of Rome. He'll say something else after, we'll get to that, but right now the important thing is this phrase. Who awakens guilt in the people of Rome? Flavius, of course. And what are the Roman people guilty of? According to the tribunes, of celebrating the assassination of Pompey.

"Now: since the tribunes are followers of Pompey, and since not too many pages ahead they are the very ones who will drive their daggers into Julius Caesar's body, where is the virtue invoked by guilt's gag rule? Flavius doesn't charge the Roman people with cheering a murderer, but rather that murderer in particular. Is it cynicism that Flavius reveals, then? Does he have a selective morality that approves of certain crimes while condemning others? I wouldn't go that far. Rather, it seems to me that the play is hostage to contingency, that swamp where ethos is diluted and leaves the door ajar in the face of atrocity."

Eighty-Three

The old Sherpa takes pride, in a manner that is altogether unjustified – it must be said – in his colleague's professional performance. He feels at once like a factotum and a sentry overseeing the progress of his – protégé? adopted son? – on that path that leads to higher education.

That is why he allows himself, from time to time, to advise him on his future with sincerity. Like that time when the young Sherpa suggested the possibility of studying the History of Law. He could have been dismissive, let it go. But no: he accepted his role of mentor. He spoke to him of Proudhon, Bakunin, and inheritance; of Amazonian tribes, young Marx and Thomas More. He told him to look around him, to appreciate the immensity of the natural oeuvre, not to waste time dismantling the mechanisms of surplus value, told him not to look down on his own tradition, to appreciate his privileges. To think twice about it, and then a third time. To keep him posted.

Something of that conversation comes back now, when he hears the young man say:

'It could have been the sun, a reflection.'

Because he understands that in that search for excuses there is also respect.

To Tell the Truth

Eleven years after the conquest of Everest, Tenzing Norgay participates in a television panel show in the United States: *To Tell the Truth*. Instead of being a panellist on the show, Norgay is a pawn. The challenge is this: Norgay and two other physiognomically similar persons appear before the four competitors (all Caucasian, all somehow anachronistic, dental). The panellists' mission is to guess which of the three Asians is the real Sherpa; which is, in fact, the man who was the first to reach the summit of Mount Everest. To conduct their investigation, each has one minute to question Norgay and the two imposters, who have been taught by the show's production team about Everest, the 1953 expedition, the life of the Dalai Lama and some other titbits of general cultural relevance. After their round of questions, the panellists venture an answer.

The contest ends: Norgay stands and reveals his identity. The two imposters also confess their real names and their occupations. One is the Indian Consul in New York; the other, the head bartender of a restaurant called the Luau 400. Only one of the contestants managed to identify the real Sherpa; he receives the prize.

Eighty-Five

'Hence! Home, you idle creatures, get you home! Is this a holiday? What, know you not, being mechanical, you ought not walk upon a labouring day without the sign of your profession? Speak, what trade art thou?'

With that announcement by Flavius, aggressive and superior, demanding and imperious, the young Sherpa has to inaugurate, upon the stage of the school's assembly hall, the representation of *Julius Caesar*. There's about a month left before that happens. And Flavius has only five interventions. It is nothing, for example, compared with the hundred lines that one of his companions has to memorise to play the role of Brutus. But that's no consolation, either. It is the young Sherpa who has to face the public the second the curtain is drawn.

Although, seen more clearly, the problem is not so much that in the third week of June the school adaptation of an Elizabethan play must be presented in public in the assembly hall of a public school lost in the Nepalese mountain range, nor that it is, precisely, the young Sherpa who must open his mouth before anyone else in order to say: 'Hence! Home, you idle creatures, get you home!' The problem is what to do after.

Tactics

What is the tactical value of the mountain? It isn't a question of strategy – long-termism is of no interest in this case. Nor of geopolitical value. It is not now a question of determining whether the mountains are coveted by the aristocracies of the world. (Once they sought fertile land. Then mineral deposits, hydrocarbons, potable water, desperate demographics, subjectivities.) The only question is a military one. Is it better to attack from the mountain? Or is it the ideal site for resistance? Why are mountains avoided as battlefields? Why is the open field preferred? Where are the great battles waged? In valleys, alongside rivers, perhaps in some North African desert, or on the fluctuating surface of the oceans. Before city walls, on bridges… This is a shame. The mountains would be an excellent setting for guerrilla warfare. Not the tropical mountains: heat, insects, malaria, humidity. The mountain. Infertile, uncovered, exposed; uncomfortable. This very mountain where the young Sherpa looks at the old Sherpa and is on the verge of asking him: 'What if we throw a pebble at him?' But he decides to keep quiet.

Impressionist Painters

If the two Sherpas were Impressionist painters, the older man would be Renoir, and the younger Monet.

In 1869, both of them – Monet, Renoir – were still poor, and no one had ever uttered the word *impressionism*. One day they arrange to meet in La Grenouillère, quite a small town some seventy kilometres from Paris. A sort of seaside resort with no sea where the bourgeois go for their recreation in the summer. On a bend in the Seine, the vital forces of La Grenouillère had managed to lend the town an identity: a summer escape close to the metropolis, but just far enough to detach from the gravitation of flourishing capitalism and the fetid vapours still expelled by the cadaver of the *Ancien Régime* almost a century after its death.

How or why Monet and Renoir decide to paint the same thing is not known. In a letter to Frédéric Bazille, then a pre-Impressionist painter himself, Monet writes: 'I have a dream: a painting, the bathers at La Grenouillère. I've already done some bad sketches, but it's just a dream. Renoir, who has been here for two months, also wants to paint the same picture.' A year after receiving this letter, Bazille enlisted in a Zouave regiment, went to fight against the Prussians, surrounded by descendants of Algerians, and died in battle.

But it isn't the tragedy of Bazille that is directly and intensely linked to the two Sherpas who are watching an Englishman on the mountain, but rather Renoir and Monet. The two artists who now put their easels next to each other choose a similar point of view and begin. Impressionists paint quickly. That's a policy of theirs. Speed. A charm that prefigures industrialisation. They don't take long to finish their canvases or to compare their works.

Neither one of them is a wonder. Neither Monet nor Renoir has reached full maturity. Impressionism is just now taking its first steps. It does not yet have a bed, or banks, or a direction. It only barely has any tributaries. From one side, Delacroix and his progressive abandonment of the dictatorship of the plane in favour of the body of the brushstroke; his contempt for Neoclassicism. His most famous work, *Liberty Leading the People*, may not be a good example. But *Horse Frightened by a Thunderstorm* is a breakthrough work: the clouds, ominous and without outlines, a bolt of lightning, a few zigs and zags that are nothing but light, the deformity of the terrified white equine, the contortion of his neck… The entire painting is a challenge. From the other side, we have Courbet and his realism, his contempt for just about everything. In this case, it is worth pausing on his most famous work: *The Origin of the World*. A naked woman lying down. A woman whose face and feet are out of the frame. A woman's body between breasts and thighs; and, in the centre of the canvas, the cunt. In the forest of foregrounds, taking exclusive priority. There are sheets in the painting, nipples, a belly button. But no one doubts that it is the portrait of a cunt. *Épater le bourgeois* circa 1866: the painting remains almost hidden for a century. It is first purchased by a fan living in Montmartre, then by an antiques dealer, then it ends up in a gallery. There it is bought by a Hungarian baron with artistic pretences, who takes it to Budapest. It becomes part of his private collection, but only until the city is occupied by the Nazi army, which seizes it and notes it down in the inventory of their looting. At the end of the war, the Red Army finds the painting and returns it to the Magyar aristocrat. Jumping the iron curtain, the baron settles in Paris, returning the painting to its native land. At auction, he sells his Courbet for one and a half million francs. The buyer: Jacques Lacan, who secretly takes the painting to his country home. Lacan keeps the painting until his death. Finally, the French State takes it for itself as a down payment on the inheritance taxes and hangs it in the Musée d'Orsay, in 1995, where it can still be seen today.

But nor is it *The Origin of the World*, or Courbet, or Delacroix, that forms the radical and pristine link with the two Sherpas who are peering into the abyss of the Himalayas; rather, it is Monet and Renoir. We must place our focus on the simultaneous contemplation of their two canvases. Two works that – by mutual agreement, it would appear – their creators title almost identically. Monet calls his *Bain à La Grenouillère*; Renoir, just *La Grenouillère*. Two minor works, it must be repeated, by two titans of nineteenth-century art. The contemplation, then, not of the two images, but rather of that simultaneous contemplation. Or perhaps not simultaneous, but at least alternating, oscillating. Until a third image is born from the consecutive vision of these two paintings painted on the same day in the same place and before the same landscape.

In the distance, a century and a half away, what is interesting about these pieces is their conversation. The two pictures don't look that different from each other at first glance. In both, a group of bourgeois enjoys a summer day along a river. On the right, a sort of gazebo that is nothing other than the outer gallery of a floating café, the most profitable business and the main attraction of La Grenouillère. From there, a footbridge connects the café with an islet. A dozen people dispense with civility under the only tree on that little Elba, or Saint Helena: all islands are important to the rise of the French bourgeoisie. On the left, a group of bathers with naked torsos swim in the river. In the foreground, an inarticulate set of boats, a concise river armada, more like a tourist fleet, ephemeral, adrift. In the background, a line of trees mark the edge of the river. Lindens, we might say, if we were being guided by Renoir's gaze. Poplars per Monet.

It is obvious that in Renoir's work there is a greater degree of detail: the hats of the gentlemen can be distinguished, the bows that encircle the women's waists, the parasols the girls carry that enliven the riverbanks in the midsummer heat... The colouring of the painting decants into half a dozen shades of green. Renoir is delicate. He would like to be fully impressionistic, but he's too delicate. There seems to be an effort to brutalise his brushwork in this painting. An effort evidently insufficient. It's not enough for him to twist the mimetic direction of Western tradition. There's something that's stronger than he is. He is, against his will, overly adapted.

Monet's picture, on the other hand, is nothing but splotches. Yes, that is a leg, and that is a bather looking out at the water, and that must be the short bridge that leads to the islet. Yes, it can all be understood. But that doesn't make them anything but splotches. Yellow and sky blue, and largely black (though some furiously red diagonals give their all in the lower righthand corner, from the edge of a little boat). Splotches: impressionist euphemism once launched at the speed of modern art. The canvas no longer serves a cartographic purpose: it seeks not to miniaturise the hollow of the perceptible. Heuristic rather than mimetic, the brush is unleashed and, in that liberating gesture, it becomes a bit solipsistic.

Flabbier, less lucid, but also friendlier, Renoir's painting preserves the deliberate effort to leave a testimony to the spirit of the age: the clothes of the bourgeoisie, their hairstyles, what they ate and drank. A panegyric on the new era. He even paints a scantily clad servant carrying a tray of refreshments to the bathers. Following the inspiration of Baudelaire, that generation's mainstay, Renoir acts as a portraitist of modern life. He thus establishes a relationship with his historical locus. Renoir wants to be a chronicler. With religious images and mythological hyperbole in exile, he is able to paint what he sees.

Meanwhile, in Monet's work there is one obsession: light. Each component of the painting is an excuse to establish a new anchor point in that unfinished argument between Monet and light. He is motivated by the debate on the possibilities of art. He doesn't claim to paint portraits, to immortalise what stands before his eyes, but rather an idea, a concept, a capacity for expanding the bounds of representation to the point of ripping it apart and leaving it for dead. They will have killed it soon. And representation will be reborn. Three days later. And they will put on another crucifixion. But it will be back. And so on, all the time. Until it becomes boring, pointless.

But for now, Monet and Renoir swap places, study each other's paintings; let us assume they praise each other. Then they fold up their easels, put away their tubes, wash off their brushes and return to Paris. Twenty, eighty, a hundred and fifty years pass. Two Sherpas look down; an Englishman, his body still. The two Sherpas look down on the nadir while Monet's painting hangs on a wall in

New York's Metropolitan Museum, on Fifth Avenue, and Renoir's painting is shown at the Nationalmuseum of Stockholm, 6,300 kilometres apart.

Eighty-Eight

Three days after the Sherpa assembly and six after the avalanche of fourteen thousand tons of ice and snow, the representatives of the Nepali government arrived at Base Camp. The delegation was headed by the Minister of Culture, Tourism and Civil Aviation. He met with the Sherpas. He tried to convince them to go back up. He made promises. The strikers experienced a moment's hesitation. They agreed to meet again to advance the dialogue. As the retinue of functionaries was about to depart in their helicopter, a dull rumour arrived at the camp from the west side of the mountain: another avalanche. Explicit *kan runu* in the middle of the union's uprising. The Sherpas called an urgent closed-door meeting. It was decided. There would be no more ascents for the remainder of that season.

Eighty-Nine

The old Sherpa often wonders what he would do with the mountain if he were in charge. Here an objection might be raised: what does he mean when he says *in charge*? How could he be in charge of a mountain? The phrase doesn't have a hermetic meaning in this case. He means, without any big mystery, that he would be responsible for, and at the same time, the only one able to make, decisions about what happens on Mount Everest. Does a mountain meet the requirements for someone to be put in charge of it? What can be done with a mountain? Besides climbing it, of course. At this point, the old man would reply that the possibilities are infinite. He'd be exaggerating (because there aren't that many), but he'd enumerate: the mountain could be closed to preserve it in its current state; the mountain could be commercially exploited in a thousand different ways; or it might be drilled in order to extract some mineral resource from it, might be transformed into the planet's largest system of wormholes. Copper, silver, lithium – who knows what might be found? Or its usefulness for tourism might be enhanced: you could build four or five resorts... something big, with heated pools, Jacuzzis, timeshares... But, of course, all these possibilities seem atrocious to him.

So what would the old Sherpa do with the mountain if he were in charge? He has already decided: if he were responsible for Mount Everest, he would give it to the Sherpas. There's nobody who'd take better care of it. *Nobody better than us*, he thinks. All the power to the Sherpas. He'd allow them to conduct tourism, hiking, whatever they'd consider appropriate. Hang gliding? Skiing? Sure, whatever the Sherpas decide. They'd never harm the giantess.

Of course – the old Sherpa qualifies – you would have to require of the tourists and of the Sherpas themselves that they comply with certain basic conditions, minimal infrastructural norms, maintenance of the environment, hygiene... But, in that case, again it seems apt to ask how a control system would be put in place in order to ensure that those elemental rules of coexistence in the mountain would be followed. Because there is always the possibility that the implementation of this utopia, of this phalanstery on high, might find itself blocked by negligence, by greed, by inefficiency, by simple, stupid spite. Thus it is necessary to establish a contingency plan, extra insurance in case someone breaches the pact. That much is obvious. But the old Sherpa has already figured it out: at the slightest incident, he would blow up the mountain with the largest load of dynamite in the history of the world.

If the young Sherpa knew of these ideas of the older man's, he would reply with a dazzling smile: 'Dynamite? How old-fashioned!'

Ninety

Once enthroned as the first man to ever set foot on the summit of Everest, Edmund Hillary becomes a professional adventurer. With a certain phlegmatic desperation, he sets out to climb ten more Himalayan peaks; he succeeds. It's not enough. He joins an overland expedition to the South Pole; he reaches the meeting point of the meridians. It's not enough. He gets married, he has three children. His wife and one of the girls are killed in a plane crash in Kathmandu, in the foothills of the mountain range. He marries the widow of a friend. It's not enough. He sets up a complex charitable enterprise for the benefit of the Sherpa population. He founds schools and hospitals in remote villages of Nepal. It's not enough. He receives eleven decorations: from the British, the New Zealanders, the Nepalis, the Indians, the Poles… It's not enough. He dies of a heart attack. They name an airport after him.

Ninety-One

The young Sherpa, in order to radiate empathy with the world, looks at his partner and points down. The gesture refers to the Englishman, of course. To his situation. If indeed it refers to something. Then he sits down beside the older man with the intention of conversing with him. About anything, like two friends who no longer have too much to say to one another and who only speak of the contingent. He tries to say something about the proximity, altogether urgent, of the night.

'What about when it gets dark?' asks the young man.

'In five minutes we'll call Base Camp.'

A Woman Nurses her Child

Right now (which is to say: before), the old Sherpa is walking, comprehending that you do not always need to give an explanation. As he covers the peninsula, he resolves not to justify himself at once. He greets Rabbit from afar and then continues to get closer. She sees him coming, of course; but she seems to be more concerned not to give up on the mechanised movements with which she is cradling the baby. The blind dog howls two or three times, but it is clear that it is merely an alarm system, and not a reprisal. He howls and sprawls out on the grass. But then he thinks again, regrets it: he gets up and walks away. If the advance of the stranger has to lead to a full-blown attack, he would prefer to be elsewhere rather than fall prey to the idea that he was unable to defend his territory. The old Sherpa smiles and, from time to time, lifts his hand as he walks. Less and less: the greeting loses emphasis as the distance between them shrinks. Rabbit doesn't return the greeting, but nor is her expression hostile. Nor is it especially curious. It is, rather, the gesturality of slight annoyance: someone who has to face a minor obstacle, a routine inconvenience. As if she'd just returned from the pharmacy and realised she had to go back out again to buy fungicide. And so the seconds pass. Just a few seconds. Until someone has to speak:

'Hi, how are you.'

'Hi. Can I help you?'

'Is he yours?'

The Sherpa points an index finger at the baby. He doesn't understand that there are few things more terrifying than a young man who shows up alone, aimlessly walking cross country, and points at a nursing infant to inquire after his stock. For this reason, Rabbit withdraws, assumes a defensive position.

'Do I know you?'

The Sherpa senses her fear and feels doubly mortified.

'Yes, no. No, you do not know me. We crossed paths but didn't…'

'Crossed paths?'

Out of instinct, Rabbit takes a step back. The baby expresses something. A syllable, let's call it. Less: a nasal vowel. It isn't crying, no. It's more of a reaffirmation. Like someone who might say with petulance: 'Yes, here I am, cast into the world, and because I am here, I proclaim my being and demand that those responsible for this unconsulted casting preserve my existence.' The Sherpa takes note. You don't always need to give an explanation, true; but opacity is overly revealing. You see everything. He elects to polish.

'At the corner store… At the supermarket, the grocery – I don't know how you say it here…'

A silence.

'You were crying? Remember?'

It was enough to press that key. Now, slowly, inspired, without disturbing the reigning being that was the baby, a quiet cry comes out of Rabbit once again. And from this new cry, all speeds up. Rabbit disarms. She clings to the baby. The Sherpa feels the double edge of compassion and power: he doesn't want her to cry; he knows that he was the one who made her cry this time. And so he dissolves into apologies. That he didn't want to be a bother, that he only came to see if there was something he could help her with, that in the store he thought she seemed like she was doing so very badly that he felt a little selfish for leaving without asking, and that if she wants he can come back some other time or not come back at all. That it was clumsy of him to come here unannounced. Then she makes her penultimate move. She turns, goes back in the house, and leaves the door open.

'Come in.'

That's what Rabbit says. And disappears into that half-darkness of rooms that are closed on summer afternoons. The old Sherpa – what else is he going to do? – follows.

The house is predictably simple on the inside, too. One room that combines dining, kitchen, sitting and pantry. Table, four chairs – one broken – a two-seater settee, an aluminium countertop, two burners, the refrigerator, a cupboard resting on the floor. And more things: a proliferation of the inanimate. A snorkel, a rake, a basin, two bags of dog food, a changing table, and more things. A high chair: Rabbit sits her child in it. The baby smacks the plastic tray with both fat palms. He is frenzied. In the back of the room, the Sherpa sees a short hallway and three doors. Two bedrooms and a bathroom, he infers.

But that isn't what stands out most on this panoramic scan. That is the cortex. The nucleus is the two-seater settee, occupied by a man. Seated, immobile, staring straight ahead, as though hypnotised by a Caribbean telethon. As if he had decided not to blink until he uncovered the figurative key concealed in a Jackson Pollock painting. A man.

'My husband.'

The old Sherpa inclines his head with considerable courtesy and says hello.

'How are you, nice to meet you.'

There's no response. Nothing. Not even a nasty face. Not even the flicker of lateral perception in the contour of the corneas.

A young woman nurses her child. Now the old Sherpa knows: her name is Rabbit. She is in her house; almost a shack, a hut. Outside it's clear, the sky. The baby is growing fast and disproportionately. His ears are too big for that head. His hands are very small in relation to his feet. The young mother knows this and is restless. She says, from time to time: 'Aren't those tiny hands adorable?' Or, later on: 'Those ears come from his father's side; in my family no one has those ears.'

His father. The old Sherpa is particularly concerned about that father. The man who is sitting on the settee, totally absorbed in nothing.

Rabbit goes on: 'It's not that I think my baby's ugly. He's sweet, he's precious. But I'm worried he's not growing right.' In some paradoxical way, that thought reassures her. It drives off any notion of rejection and sends her towards optimistic conclusions. 'It's going to be okay. His father is a very attractive man,' she says, swollen with maternity, raising the child to be able to examine him better. The father: that creature who is extinguishing himself immobile on his seat, without any response to stimuli, without expressing more than an endemic incapacity.

His heir burps, rolls his eyes, dribbles a trickle of drool from his gums. Rabbit calls the baby by his name;

mother and son look into each other's eyes, in a kind of communion that can only be achieved by two people who have shared an umbilical cord. They look at each other and smile, the little baby with his overgrown ears and his mother, beautiful, innocent.

A cloud, the only cloud in an otherwise clear sky, crosses the path of the sun, and the light gets, all of a sudden, grey, faded. Rabbit seizes the opportunity to go into one of the bedrooms and lay the baby down in his crib. When she comes back into the living room, she puts a kettle on the fire and opens the windows so the house will air out. 'That's what my mother used to say: the house has to breathe,' she explains to the old Sherpa.

The draught brings with it some optimism. The old Sherpa is excited by the possibility that the spell will be broken, and the father of the child will abandon his suspension. That he will stop concentrating on his introspective shock. But nothing happens. 'As everybody knows,' Rabbit is telling the old Sherpa, 'my mother could do everything.' She doesn't mean that, of course. She isn't alluding to omnipotence. She means, rather, that there was no domestic challenge that her mother couldn't tame. Stains on clothes, dust on furniture, food preservation. 'She knew all the secrets you need to keep a household running.' Rabbit explains to the Sherpa that, even as a child, she admired her mother's skill and cease-lessly divulged this idolatry. That was why her family's army of satellites gave her little toy feather dusters and party-favour brooms. So that, through early emulation, little Rabbit could become, someday, an efficient manager of her home and a meticulous administrator of her garden.

As the plot lines expand, three ideas compete for a monopoly over the old Sherpa's consciousness. The first has to do with submission to stereotypes. The second with the attraction he feels towards Rabbit, even with her husband four and a half metres away, lost in thought and a prisoner of the most hermetic silence. The third, it is evident, revolves around Rabbit's omissions: why does she tell him in such a detailed way about her mother's life and not explain anything that has to do with that man in his vegetative state, in the very same room they are, staring at the wallpaper?

Then, little by little, over the years – Rabbit is explaining to him – the tasks of the household ceased to be a priority for her. Her mother noted that she no longer ran up to hold her dustpan when she swept the hallway, that she no longer went out of her way to dry the dishes that emerged immaculate from the sink. She still helped, of course. But her enthusiasm diminished with every passing day, until it could be said that she did it reluctantly. In any case, her parents connected it with the inevitable, but fleeting, stage of puberty. Bigger was the surprise the day her mother had to go up to Rabbit's room and ask her to please come down to the dining room to set the table, an activity that – what is more – she had always jealously reserved for herself. Now in full adolescence, Rabbit carried out with obedience and tedium the household chores that her strict mother would impose on her. Of course, as she made the beds or hung the clothes on the line, she could not stop whimpering or, and this was more common, crying her eyes out, repeating (not always just to herself) the unhappiness she felt when she was chained to a mop or a floor squeegee. How unjust God had been to arrange nature in such an unhygienic manner, requiring daily adjustments to put back on track what, left to its own devices, would wind up a gigantic rubbish tip, an enormous ocean of scourges and diseases and filth.

In any case, it would never have occurred to Rabbit to question her mother's orders, perhaps intimidated by the severe figure of this woman who had transformed her home into an infallible mechanism of precision, a Prussian hourglass. So that – as she herself tells the old Sherpa – Rabbit grew up cleaning and scrubbing, sweeping and washing, until one Easter Sunday she fainted while polishing the crystal beads on the old lamp in the dining room. When she regained consciousness, she was in her bed with a headache; a doctor was talking to her mother behind the door. He was telling her that heavy chores would be out of the question from that day forward. The only thing that mattered was rest. And fresh air, running, and hiding things.

Rabbit – she says it herself now, in the sitting room, while the baby sleeps in his room, and the man of the house sits entrenched on the settee, petrified – she wanted to continue listening to the doctor, but it was making her sleepy. Her eyes kept closing. Before falling asleep, she thought for the first time that she would like to live in a hotel, a place where every day someone would come to tidy up your room for you, make your bed, spray a pine-scented freshener in the bathroom. A hotel with an elegant reception area, circular, where the reading chairs were crowded around mahogany coffee tables. Where the concierge would know her name, where he would transfer phone calls to her room: 'señora Rabbit, your mother's on the phone, shall I put her through?' It is what she refers to as – always as the most shameful of secrets, she clarifies – the *hotel fantasy*. 'It's the first time I've ever told anyone,' she confesses to the old Sherpa. He finds this hard to believe. It strikes him as something she probably tells everyone, all the time.

The Sherpa understands, after a while, that there isn't much left for him to do. The baby is sleeping, the man is watching the wallpaper, Rabbit is talking without any pause. She's pretty, and she talks without breathing, serves tea, moves her hands on the tablecloth, but says nothing about the man who watches the wallpaper while the baby sleeps. Everything seems stable. The dog had briefly disrupted the slackness of the canvas. He had come in with his blindness in tow, wagging his tail and demanding attention. But he had immediately taken on the sepia tones of the whole: he stretched out next to the settee and is now dreaming a bit of outdated images, lacking in colour, and another bit of strong aromas. He looks like, although nobody notices it, the dog that presides over Velázquez's *Las Meninas*. In any case, the scene dies down; the old Sherpa decides it is time for him to leave.

'Well…'

He says that, and the word leaves its harmonics bouncing off the walls of the room. The old Sherpa announces his withdrawal; it's a *well* of transition. If it were winter, the expression would arrive in the company of a gesture: casting around for his coat, rubbing his hands together, slapping his knees. Summer is more merciless: it leaves everything to orality. The Sherpa, for a moment, misses the cold. He gets up and gets distracted. Cold without snow. Cold that encourages you to dissipate your energy reserves. No more concentration of powers, but rather survival and fuel. He gets distracted, or bored: He thinks of the gloomy fruit carts that are parked in front of his house on the harshest day of winter. They stop, they exhibit their wares without flies, with freshness. Pears, peaches, melons – all sweet, all ready. How is that possible? the old Sherpa wonders: ripe fruit while the cruel north wind blows? He gets distracted, or sleepy. The salesman looks at him. Moves his head: Are you

240

going to buy something or what? No, not this time. Tomorrow, maybe, when noon is less ubiquitous. When the pale winter sun takes some licence in its metre. Then, perhaps, a fruit. A watermelon, to choose the biggest in the cart. So that you understand that it's not a matter of financial or seasonal problems. A whole watermelon, unsliced. I'll reserve for myself the revealing incision. What's the problem? The Sherpa is distracted, is bored. Already plotting his escape.

Rabbit, on the other hand, tenses:

'Are you leaving?'

The Sherpa is surprised. His world was already a different world. It was winter, and there was tropical fruit. Not this heat and this question. The blind dog wakes up: it lifts one of its ears. The Sherpa, standing, tries a deep breath and nods. That double gesture, which he arbitrarily associates with the most withering determination, is still available to him on this scorching summer day. Rabbit seems on the verge of saying something. She raises a hand. But the voice to be heard comes from the other direction. Without taking his eyes off the wallpaper, the man, at last, now speaks:

'The Ministry of War sent a newly weaned puppy to the family of every dead soldier.'

The voice is grave; its cadence spacious. The gaze remains fixed to the wallpaper. Everything is, for a moment, suspended.

'A little puppy, yes. For every dead soldier.'

Rabbit's husband has spoken, and everything is in a state of exception. The Sherpa sets aside his eagerness to escape. The dog lifts his other ear. They both look at the man who has spoken. Rabbit, too, who interrupts her gesture (hand raised to stop the avalanche) to instantly

241

run to her husband, to squat down next to him, put a hand on his left thigh.

'Hello, my love, it's me. What were you saying?'

But the man is no longer speaking. He has tumbled back into silence. Rabbit's tear ducts turn red again, and she lets a moment pass and then removes her limp hand from his lap, gently. She takes a moment to listen to the lack of a response. She straightens up, observes the old Sherpa and his disconcertedness. She goes up to him, takes his arm, guides him slowly out the door, out of the house, and she starts to cry. Again, Rabbit cries. The Sherpa sees the fingers of the weeper on his arm. A bit of pressure on his skin, the muscles, a tendon. He doesn't dislike it.

'What war is he talking about?'

The old Sherpa sympathises, of course. But he's also curious.

'No war. I don't know. He's never been in any war. He's never left this town…'

The old Sherpa concedes: you don't always have to explain yourself, but nor can every single thing be understood. Rabbit still has him by the arm, still gazing up at him with watery eyes. He has expressed his sympathy aloud. Sadness – attractive, impalpable – becomes intelligible to him. Not so the troubled well of the man who's still sitting in front of the wallpaper, back inside the house. But not everything can be understood, he accepts again.

'I understand.'

That's what he says at the edge of the peninsula. It doesn't mean he understands the core. Only that the man on the two-seater settee is immersed in a war that, in addition to being non-existent, is already lost. And he understands that this defeat spreads its influence over the

rest of the house: Rabbit, the baby, the snorkel, the blind
dog, the basin… But she says something, too.

'Could I ask you a favour? A big favour?'

Rabbit speaks. Worse: asks. A favour, she asks. And it is
as though the women were passing. The ones that look,
or hold his gaze, so that the old Sherpa feels that he is
little, almost nothing; so that he looks at his ankles, barely
grazed by dark algae, there, in the ocean, on holiday, if
holidays still exist. There where the tenuous current that
returns, the wet sand and its roughness tell of the regur-
gitating of the oceanic mass.

The dialogue is asymmetrical. The old Sherpa doesn't say
much. He nods more than anything. Rabbit, meanwhile,
goes on. She promises him that it will only be three
hours, maybe four, between when she leaves and when
she comes back from the store; she shows him the bottles
filled with breast milk on the shelves of the refrigerator,
the little pot to heat up the bottles in; she shows him
the bags of nappies, the changing table; she dissolves into
expressions of gratitude, tears; she warns him about the
importance of burping, praises the properties of oleo-cal-
careous liniment; she tells him about two women neighbours, both of them elderly and half deaf, who might in
the worst-case scenario help him out in an emergency;
she assures him he will receive innumerable heavenly
blessings in return for being so good; she tells him that
she feels very ashamed, repeating several times that she has
no other way out, but she swears that she will resolve her
work situation in a more sustainable way, that she is just
about to figure it out; she explains to him the maternity
leave regime, and she starts to tear up again, or to weep
mournfully; she advises him not to worry about the dog,
who can take care of himself, nor about her husband,

who is still frozen, elbows on his lap, eyes on the wall; she kisses him on the cheek; she says – retrospectively – that if she keeps going like this she will be fired from her job; and she leaves, she gets on her bike, she heads for the sea; she leaves the old Sherpa standing there, in the middle of the room, three metres from the wallpaper man and four from the baby, who is still sleeping. Why was it that Rabbit was crying?

Roman Thesis

"There is a final speech by Flavius before he disappears forever from the play and from history. His legacy, in some sense. It starts with an order to Marullus. He asks him to go to the Capitol and, on his way, to strip the statues of the ornaments that celebrate the triumph of Julius Caesar. Marullus, with sudden prudence, asks him: 'May we do so? You know it is the feast of Lupercal.' His fear is justified. There is a political and religious prohibition against vandalising the images of Rome. Nonetheless, Flavius responds: 'It is no matter.' His terror of Julius is so great that he no longer fears the gods. He will finish his lines with an ornithological metaphor. 'These growing feathers plucked from Caesar's wing will make him fly an ordinary pitch, who else would soar above the view of men and keep us all in servile fearfulness,' he'll say. But before that, before pronouncing his final word, he leaves a promise and an entreaty: 'I'll about and drive away the vulgar from the streets; So do you too, where you perceive them thick.'

"Why does Flavius hate Caesar so much? Or does he hate the vulgar? What if Rome's only options were ominous plutocracy and centripetal tyranny? Would you,

young Himalayan actor, welcome with cheers the arrival
of the barbarian hordes, the sack and robbery?"

Ninety-Four

'In five minutes we'll call Base Camp.'

The older man responds and looks up to confirm the position of the sun. It seems that this evasive gesture is all he can articulate, in the end, about the role of chance and topography in the survival of the species. Then he kicks a rock, which is like kicking the whole mountain.

Ninety-Five

Half a century has passed since the conquest of Everest. Tenzing has been dead for seventeen years. Hillary more than five. The summit has received some 4,000 visits in five decades: an average of eighty per year. The mother of the world has lost her exclusivity; the mystique – latent or manifest – of all sectarianism has been blurred.

Yaks

Another time – as we were saying – a year and a week after the avalanche of fourteen thousand tons of ice and snow, Nepal is the epicentre of an earthquake that measures 7.8 on the Richter scale. That day, 8,700 people die. More than nine million Nepali people, a third of the population, require assistance. Half the country is left without a place to live, without potable water, medical infrastructure, electricity, any means of communication…

That day, as the crisis erupts, Nima Chhiring, the Sherpa with the crying ear, is on the mountain. Almost against his will. After the avalanche and the strike, he had vowed never to cross the threshold of Everest again. Yet he immediately betrayed that decision. He has a wife and two school-aged children. With no home of his own, or any other vocation to offer to the restrictive Nepali job market, the earthquake finds him once more with crampons on his boots, ice axe in hand and harness strapped to his waist. He's trying to work. But it's a tough season: few tourists dare to venture into the Himalayas after the avalanche. And now, to top it all off, the earthquake… But Nima is still there. Almost always at Base Camp, waiting. Or in Darjeeling, with his family. Watching the news about how they're trying to reconstruct Nepal. Or, at times, how they've resigned themselves to catastrophe. Accepting ruin as hypodermis, rubble as second skin. The months take their time moving on: April, June, September. Until climbing season ends. There is nothing to do in the mountains. Then, yes, at last, Nima goes home, to the home he rents, and he announces to his family that he will never work as a mountain guide again. That it's over. That he's bidding farewell to the giantess.

Nima retires with his family to the countryside. Now he's a shepherd. He has five yaks. He's trying his luck in the dairy business.

The truth is he's not doing very well.

Ninety-Seven

An idea settles provisionally in the young Sherpa's mind. What if it wasn't an accident? He's not thinking about predestination, but rather about attempted murder. He reconstructs the sequence. He was bringing up the rear; the older man was ahead; the Englishman in the middle, protected. Then came the bend, the old Sherpa turned. Then the Englishman and, for a few seconds, the landscape looked inorganic and unspoiled. He remembers being side-tracked by some thoughts about his academic future. And then right away he thought about his mother, who at that hour would be having lunch at the help desk of the Ministry for Tourism. He heard a noise and a voice. That much he knows for sure. A noise of secretive violence and a voice that was saying something: a single unintelligible word. In that moment, at that instant, he did not think anything urgent was happening. He kept walking. Two, three, five steps, and the young Sherpa, too, turned the corner. The older man was already looking down over the edge. Crawling. His gaze would have been hard to define, the muscles in his hands were tense. But the scene was easy enough to interpret: the Englishman had fallen, and the old Sherpa was moving towards the cliffside in order to corroborate his condition.

The young Sherpa remembers that his first thought was: *He didn't kill him.* Although now that he's decided to go over everything again, he wonders: *Why did I think that?* Why introduce the possibility of murder, even if it came negated? Now, since he has decided to review the episode one more time, he reasons: *What if the old man did kill him?* Is there, in fact, any way to find out? And if so, what role would he want to play in that hypothesis? Complicity or denunciation?

Our Kings

Why not luxuriant foliage or the sobriety of the plains? Why the mountain? On the peninsula, then, there is a man. A man sitting on a two-seater settee. The world is alien to him. Although suddenly he speaks. And for a second it seems like an interaction, an emerging, a showing his blowhole to the seagulls as he takes a breath. But no: it is only the foam of an underwater dialogue that remains out of reach. The detachment of an asteroid that is already orbiting a smaller planet. The hypothesis is confirmed: he is surrounded by other words. And there was a war.

On the other hand, there is a woman, but she has left. She tends towards melodrama, works as a cashier at a corner store three blocks from the beach. She is, at this particular moment, the sole breadwinner in this household. She was grasping a young man, one who would become a Sherpa in Nepal, by the arm. Asking if she could ask him a favour: a big favour, she said. Now she's gone.

There is a third element, too, that ought not to be underestimated. There is a baby. A few months old, this infant. He can't talk, can't walk, his autonomy is insignificant. For him to die, it is enough to do nothing. He'll die on his own. Now he's sleeping, but it is feasible to assume that from time to time he is awake.

The first five or six minutes, the stillness was perfect and deceiving. The old Sherpa, the wallpaper man, the baby: no one broke the statutory pact with Medusa. One in the folding chair, another on the settee, and the third in his crib. Each of them petrified by the absent gaze of the lady gorgon who was already pedalling in the direction of the corner store, towards the centre of the peninsula. Without Rabbit in the house, each of them assumed quietism as his doctrine; the exclusive contemplation of the divinity, and everything else, consequently, reduced to nothing.

But that seclusion and asceticism didn't last long. There are weaknesses, everyone knows that. The old Sherpa changed his position – a leg that wants to cross, a foot that frees itself from the pressure of its flip-flop – and the rest became movement. Medusa replaced by Pandora. The baby awake, clamouring in his half-tongue for his mother, bottles were heated up, colourful toys (luminous toys!) were thrown onto the floor, there was snack time for infants and burping and there were nappies, and songs, indifference was attempted, and then a more servile submission, there was a slight white vomit, there was jumpiness, fatigue, impotence, and, at the least expected moment, a nap that was finally taken back up again in the crib…

And that was just the half of what happened in the three hours and twenty-two minutes that the old Sherpa was in charge of Rabbit's house.

There was also a dialogue. Half of a dialogue. Or less than that: people spoke. Even less: things were said. Rabbit's husband, for example, said a number of them. But it was impossible to know who he was speaking to. The old Sherpa also said his piece. And it was impossible to determine if anyone was listening to him or if his voice stayed floating in a space of sterile significations. But there was some exchange, and some things were said, yes.

First was the wallpaper man. He said:

'We had kings; nobody cared for them.'

The old Sherpa took an interest. From the other extreme of the room, he asked out loud:

'What kings?'

And he broadened the set of questions without saying a word: Why did no one care for them? Whence such generalised repudiation? The man on the settee didn't answer. Eight minutes passed. The Sherpa gave up. He was dealing with the baby on the dining room table; he had laid him on top of the tablecloth and was rocking him to sleep. Three more minutes passed. Rabbit's husband spoke again:

'They didn't either.'

And that was it. The old Sherpa made another attempt.

'Didn't what?'

The Sherpa and his curiosity: didn't what? Didn't care for anybody? Didn't put much effort in? What? Were they cruel, were they ruthless? There was, of course, no answer.

A wardrobe was painted yellow, a blanket had a print with a merry-go-round. The baby was just about to fall asleep. Or so it seemed. The Sherpa had left him in the crib, in his room. He was feeling fairly proud of his work as a nanny. For a beginner, he had acquitted himself of this situation with quite a bit of dignity. His index finger had been captured by the infant's hand, eyes closed, wheezing. The old Sherpa sang him a lullaby. A folk song, in reality. But he was whispering it and had thereby transmuted it into a medieval lullaby. When he came to the chorus, he enjambed the words that started with y: yakety-yak, yearning, youngster... It was a relaxing ruse. He was interrupted by a voice in the distance: coming from the sitting room. The intonation was interrogative. The words had escaped him. He poked his head out. He apologised.

'I didn't quite hear you.'

'What were our kings like?'

The question was clear. Less definitive was the addressee. The man on the two-seater settee was still staring at the wall. The Sherpa wondered if it made sense to respond. He decided to do it with a question.

'Our kings?'

'Every family that lost a child was compensated with a recently weaned puppy.'

From the crib, the baby started crying.

Why the mountain? And the plateau with its arid rubble? What about the Atlantic Forest, exuberant and salt-sprayed? Later, an hour and forty minutes after Rabbit's departure, the baby was sleeping again. The man, with his elbows resting on his thighs, his unfathomable gaze on the wall, said:

'I don't know of anyone who's seen them.'

The old Sherpa didn't answer. Nevertheless, the man on the settee had more questions:

'And where did they live? There was no castle. How old were they? Were our kings children?'

The young old Sherpa yawned.

There was another period of silence. The baby was still sleeping, the wallpaper man kept quiet. The old Sherpa was distracted. He imagined the house of those two deaf old women to whom he could turn in case of domestic crisis. He imagined them twins. And insufferable. He constructed a house thrumming with senile complaints that, out of saturation, wound up a placid murmur. The overlapping of voices became harmonious, the howls of two hearing-impaired women in the mnemic twilight of their generation. They were sweet, in the end, the voices of those two women reproaching one another for the most horrendous things that happened in their childhood: no longer the breaking of a toy or parental favouritism, no longer a hateful habit or a belligerent attitude, but rather hair pulled out by the roots, little mutilations, the evisceration of pets. The old Sherpa would have liked to take refuge in the warmth of those two inseparable sisters, halves of the same ripe fruit, pretty putrid by this time, in fact, suitable for serving as a nest for worms, nursery for the children of flies.

He thought all that, or he imagined it, the old Sherpa, and meanwhile the sun had already started its descent towards the west and the yellowish light provided a crepuscular quality to Rabbit's sitting room... The man spoke from his settee:

'Did our kings care for us?'

The old Sherpa tried to think of a response. Or an expansion of the question: Did kings have desires? When it came to kings, were we dealing with an eroticised State? But he said nothing; very quietly, the man completed his penultimate question:

'Were they interested in us?'

The Sherpa decided that he would not try to further converse with the wallpaper man. But, a little bit out of guilt and a little in the interest of comfort, he sat down beside him. The settee was now full. It felt cosy, soft. Sunset was an agonising phenomenon. Its pastel hues induced a kind of lethargy. The promise of night time encumbered his eyelids. The Sherpa leaned his head against the back of the settee. He closed his eyes. He wanted to return to his musings about the deaf twins who moved in felt slippers through the corridors of the neighbouring house. He wound up thinking about Rabbit. Did he dream of her? No, it couldn't be said that he was totally asleep. At moments he was captain of orienting the course of the images in his frontal lobe. From time to time, his reverie had an autonomy.

The stage was the corner store. Behind the bakery aisle, she was waiting for him. Agitated, clandestine, excited by the potential appearance of an inopportune witness among the bags of pita bread. In the fantasy, the Sherpa acted ever so slightly discourteous at first. As though the whole situation were of no interest to him. This permitted him to be distant and at the same time dominating. A word settled in centre stage: clemency. A word evidently wrongly used. There was no clemency of any kind in this plot. There was nothing to forgive. But that word was sufficient to accelerate the progress of the sequence. There was another word that loitered around the construction of the scene: magnanimous. The old Sherpa enjoyed feeling clement and magnanimous. He pictured Rabbit small, scared, desiring. He, meanwhile, couldn't care less. It was all the same to him: turn on his heel and head out the door of the supermarket or rip apart Rabbit's thighs with her hipbones. It was all the same to him. But he was magnanimous. That was why he approached Rabbit's body in this fantasy: he standing, she (it wasn't very clear why) sitting on the floor, with her knees drawn in against her chest. And that was as far as he got. Up to proximity. He didn't care about the rest. For this reason, it was she who, from the floor, launched the sexual kinesis of getting up a little, getting on her knees and going straight for genitalia, unfastening belts and zippers with lightning speed between moans of anxiety. He did nothing. Observing from above, like someone who condescends almost tenderly to fulfil the desire of others. Like someone who lets his kids play a little bit more under the stormy skies, despite the fact that they are not allowed to. Like someone who clemently allows them to have a little more fun before ordering them to go inside the house at once, drying them off with a towel and subjecting them to the most brutal of physical punishments.

He was woken by the voice of the wallpaper man:

'Our kings… Did we figure, even if just for a moment, in their thoughts?'

That was what he said. And then he slowly listed to the right. A ship tilted by the impact of a torpedo. A boat with hulls flooded by the slow flow of the sea into its bowels. Until he was resting his head on the Sherpa's lap. And there he fell asleep.

That's how Rabbit found them. The baby in his crib, in the white unconsciousness of neonatal sleep. Her husband – he, too: closed eyes, slow breathing – with his head on the Sherpa's left thigh. The blind dog wagging his tail, striking it against the legs of the dining table. The old Sherpa himself, staring absently at the wallpaper. It was night: the lights were off.

Without speaking, almost without making any noise at all, she deposited her backpack on the table. She checked in on the baby first. She came back to the sitting room. She knelt so that her head was next to the Sherpa's knees and stroked her husband's hair. She said something into his ear. The man on the settee sat up without sudden movements. It would have been hard to say if he was embarrassed, confused, or oblivious to everything. Darkness. She took his hand and led him into the bedroom. He let himself be guided, docile, an out-of-order automaton. A being of thermoplastic polymers shuffling his feet over a planet of overwhelming gravity. The Stations of the Cross for a foam rubber messiah.

When Rabbit returned, she tried to show gratitude. She sat down on the settee in conversational spirit. Whispering, but with a predisposition for eloquence. The continuity of her actions struck the Sherpa as blatant and atrocious. They would chat, they would eat a regional cheese, they would open a bottle of wine, the polar ice caps would melt, adultery would be perpetrated. Right there: on the settee, furtively, facing the wallpaper.

On the other side of the wall, the son and the father of the son. Sleeping, not even disturbed. What if one of them woke up? Would one or the other of them, father or son, comprehend the semiotics of the sounds that would reach him from the sitting room? The touch, the rhythm, the held-back breath? And the signs come morning? Would the father, or the father's son, decode the slight disorder, the uneven sagging of the cushions, the infinitesimal spillage of the glass of wine on the coffee table? And the blind dog? What sign might his hypertrophied sense of smell perceive by nature and by adaptation?

The Sherpa wanted to leave right away. He stood and adjusted his flip-flops. He was leaving. In a straight line: as he left when the women who looked or who held his gaze would pass. Who passed and laid waste. He wanted to leave quickly. He heard Rabbit saying things to him. First next to the settee, then beside the dining table. Finally, under the doorframe. Mostly they were words of gratitude, a lukewarm offer to let him spend the night there, a mention of unpayable debts, generosity, the virtues of the Samaritans. But all was foggy in the old Sherpa's ears: he was already encircled by nimbostratus clouds, replete with water in search of condensation. A violent rain that never starts to fall. 'The sky is clear, tomorrow is going to be a nice day to go to the beach,' Rabbit said, or gave to understand, or perhaps only wished.

The Sherpa ignored the weather forecast and said goodbye. He started walking. At an absurd velocity: race walking, as they call it at the Olympics. He was surprised by how easy it was to locate the route back to the centre of the peninsula. He remembered the newly weaned puppies. He wondered when, but especially how, Rabbit's baby was conceived. He didn't know what to think. He felt uncomfortable, out of place. He noticed something bulging in his pocket. He put his hand inside. Three postcards: Stonehenge, Teotihuacán, the Himalayas.

The next day, he cut his holiday short.

Ninety-Nine

'These people... Why won't he do anything? He could cry out, at least.'

'Shall we get up?'

'Sure.'

'What if we go down?

'No. Because if I stay here...'

'True. Better not.'

'Did he move?'

'Huh?'

'I think he moved.'

'I don't think so.'

'I just thought that maybe.'

'Might have been the sun, a reflection. What about when it gets dark?'

'In five minutes we'll call Base Camp.'

One Hundred

The two Sherpas are, then, peering into the abyss. Their bodies outstretched over the rocks, hands gripping the edge of the precipice: lying in wait. Their gestures span the panoply of subtleties that aim to elude both the guilt of the executioner and the indignation of the victim.

It never rains on Mount Everest, thinks the old Sherpa, who isn't that old, nor is he properly speaking a Sherpa. *They say the conditions aren't right for it. That it can only snow*, he tries to fathom it. But he considers it a limitation. The fact that it would never rain. He personally prefers a varied climate. The more varied, the better. He likes latitudes where summer is suffocating and winter harsh. Where after light snow comes a thaw, the vortex of a hurricane and sweltering. Droughts and famines, floods and pandemics. Those are the places he likes. Biblical cities: Nineveh, Gomorrah, ancient Egypt, and its ten extortionary plagues… He might even like London, as a matter of fact, if this Englishman would make up his mind to leave this whole thing behind him, turn his head and smile. Say something friendly.

The other Sherpa is young. Now he shuts his eyes and doesn't think about anything. Until the words appear. They come from some place. Yes, he remembers now. Vividly. It's the short speeches given by Flavius, the sure-fire prose of Shakespeare: 'Home, you idle creatures, get you home!' Then he asks himself a new question: *Playwright? Why not?* He's good with words. His professors never tire of saying so. He's never written so much as a scene. It doesn't matter. He has time.

For now he has to concentrate on the urgent matter: on the immobility of the Englishman. This attitude keeps him clinging to the mountain. Perfectly still. As if he were a miniscule animal parasitising a colossal rocky being… A hushed animal, with no aspiration other than to listen to the laconic voices of two Sherpas who are contemplating him from the heights of Mount Everest. An eternal being, dying all the time while it barely perceives, up there, the abstract plane of a cloudless sky…

Concentrate on the immediate, yes. Find an origin for it, a point of departure; discard the superfluous, go back, rush up the stream of time until the moment when he saw the old man turn the corner, and then the Englishman. And, for three seconds, all was rock, snow, atmosphere. Placidity and stillness. Three, two, one… The Englishman was gone, the old Sherpa was crawling up to the ledge, and the whole scene took on an unreal and unfortunate turn.

The rest was silence; if the deafening noise of the wind ravelling over the ridges of the Himalayas can be considered silence.

Translator's Acknowledgments

The lines from Goethe's *Faust, Part II* from 'Geological Pioneers' were translated from German into English by Leopold J. Bernays in 1839.

CHARCO PRESS

Director & Editor: Carolina Orloff
Director: Samuel McDowell

www.charcopress.com

Two Sherpas was published on
80gsm Munken Premium Cream paper.

The text was designed using Bembo 11.5 and ITC Galliard.

Printed in October 2022 by TJ Books
Padstow, Cornwall, PL28 8RW using responsibly
sourced paper and environmentally-friendly adhesive.